PUFFIN

THE QUEEN'S NOSE:
HARMONY'S HOLIDAY

Harmony threw herself across the hold just in time to grab one of Dino's hands, then she tried with all her strength to hold on as the spaghetti tried to pull her down into the muddy brown stew of the canal. Dino's hand started to slip away, then was gone, and with a plop Dino was pulled down into the canal.

'No! No!' Harmony shouted.

Another book by Steve Attridge

THE QUEEN'S NOSE:
HARMONY'S RETURN

The Queen's Nose:
Harmony's Holiday

Novelization by Steve Attridge
Adapted from the screenplay by Steve Attridge
Based on the characters created by Dick King-Smith
in the original novel *The Queen's Nose*

PUFFIN BOOKS

For Jacob, and for all at Film and General

PUFFIN BOOKS

Published by the Penguin Group
Penguin Books Ltd, 27 Wrights Lane, London w8 5tz, England
Penguin Putnam Inc., 375 Hudson Street, New York, New York 10014, USA
Penguin Books Australia Ltd, Ringwood, Victoria, Australia
Penguin Books Canada Ltd, 10 Alcorn Avenue, Toronto, Ontario, Canada m4v 3b2
Penguin Books (NZ) Ltd, 182–190 Wairau Road, Auckland 10, New Zealand

Penguin Books Ltd, Registered Offices: Harmondsworth, Middlesex, England

Published in Puffin Books 1998
1 3 5 7 9 10 8 6 4 2

Puffin Film and TV Tie-in edition first published 1998

The Queen's Nose
First published by Victor Gollancz 1983
Published in Puffin Books 1985

Set in Monotype Bembo
Typeset by Rowland Phototypesetting Ltd,
Bury St Edmunds, Suffolk
Printed in England by Clays Ltd, St Ives plc

British Library Cataloguing in Publication Data
A CIP catalogue record for this book is available from the British Library

isbn 0–140–38957–1

It could have been an adventure but it was a disaster. A whole summer spent on a houseboat free of her parents had sounded like a dream holiday to Harmony Parker, but now it was real there were definite drawbacks. One was that her sister Melody was with her. Weird neighbours in the form of the Grobblers was another problem; both Mr Grobbler and his son Gus were barely human as far as Harmony was concerned. A third blight on the summer was Aunt Glenda, Mrs Parker's sister, who had reluctantly agreed to look after Harmony and Melody. For her, 'look after' apparently meant trying to starve them both to death and being constantly grumpy.

There were compensations. One was a duck Harmony had befriended and named Puddle. Another was a highly intelligent pig called Grunter with whom Harmony would have spent more time had it not been that Grunter belonged to Gus, and just to look at Gus made Harmony wanted to barf long and loud in the canal.

Despite Puddle and Grunter, things rapidly deteriorated on the boat, and they were about to erupt with surprising consequences which no one, least of all Harmony, could have guessed at. It was dinner time and, as usual, Aunt Glenda had come in from work and had forgotten to bring in any food. She was a Special Constable, among other things, and work always put thoughts of food completely out of her head.

'Food just disappears from this place since you two came to stay,' she said grumpily. 'Harmony, go and get some chips or something for supper.'

'Why me? Why can't you? Or Melody?' Harmony said, feeling a red mist starting to grow in her brain which might well ignite in a fury and destroy all in its path.

'Because you're the youngest,' Melody said with a superior look on her face.

'And it's your turn to do the washing up afterwards,' Aunt Glenda said.

'So get going. Now,' hissed Melody.

The red mist started to intensify. Why did people always pick on *her*? Why did *she* always have to run errands? Why did *she* always get the grot jobs? Why had her parents decided to go for a long holiday in Australia without her? Why did Melody have only a little more intelligence than a beefburger? Harmony wished she had a bomb in her hand. She'd turn this place to matchwood.

There was a sudden tremor in the air and the boat rocked slightly. Then a bolt of lightning splintered light through the windows and thunder cracked. Harmony was convinced her anger had caused it. Plates rattled and pots and pans jangled and clattered in the sink.

Melody looked frightened and gripped the table. The power of my mind is awesome, Harmony thought, but then the racket stopped and she knew she was not the cause. Something odd was, but not her.

Aunt Glenda, usually unimpressed by anything, looked around. 'What on earth was that?' she asked no one in particular.

'End of the world, with any luck,' Harmony said, her bad mood somehow intensified by the strange and suddenly thundery air.

'Why are young people always so moody?' Aunt Glenda asked.

'Because old duffers make them that way,' Harmony said, and stamped off to her room.

On the boat the sisters shared a small room with bunk beds. Much to Melody's disgust, Puddle the duck slept in a basket by Harmony. Her glittery eyes watched as Harmony flopped on the lower bunk and sighed. Much as Harmony loved Puddle, even she had to admit that occasionally Puddle was not the sweetest smelling of companions, especially after a large meal. With a satisfied *phut!* Puddle settled down in her basket, apparently oblivious to the noxious pong she had just emitted.

Harmony held her nose and got up to open the porthole window. A message had been scrawled in the condensation: GO AWAY. GET LOS. THIS IS MY PLAYCE.

Harmony examined the writing, then turned to Puddle.

'Who did this, Puds?'

Puddle quacked. She had no idea.

'Maybe Gus. No, he's completely illiterate. Obviously a child wrote it. Looks like someone wishes . . .'

Her words were interrupted by another tremor, and the whole boat rocked, as if accidently knocked by a giant hand.

'Quack!' Puddle exclaimed in alarm.

'There is something pretty weird going on here,' Harmony said, sweeping up Puddle to comfort her. A shadow seemed to pass across the room, darkening the small dressing-table mirror. As Harmony looked at it, she could see the window reflected in it, and the writing erased itself. If Harmony had not been so intensely curious about what was happening she would have been frightened.

The rumblings and thunderings stopped, but for the rest of the evening there was a strange atmosphere aboard the boat. Melody couldn't stand it, so she went for a walk in the hope that she might find some decent boys. However, the canal area was not well known for decent boys, and she spent a miserable hour looking at the debris floating in the canal and wishing she could win the lottery. On the boat Aunt Glenda, not one easily spooked, was definitely getting spooked. She had a sense of being watched. She closed drawers and found them open again. She put things down and then found they had moved if she left the room and returned.

'Are you trying to drive me mad?' she asked Harmony.

'Why waste time on something that's already happened?' Harmony countered. 'You're meant to be the big police cheese. You find out what's going on.'

That night Harmony lay on the bottom bunk playing chess against herself. She liked to do this because she always won. Melody was on the top bunk, asleep and dreaming of Tom Cruise. Aunt Glenda was asleep in the next room, dreaming of becoming a Chief Inspector of Police. Puddle dozed and dreamed of having a whole lake all to herself and a personal groom for her feathers. Harmony was just about to use the white knight to put herself in check, when she heard a noise, a small fluttering noise somewhere on the boat, as if some nimble-footed animal was aboard. A rat, perhaps. She looked up, then took a small pocket torch from the bedside table and went to investigate.

She shone the torch across the kitchen to reveal unwashed plates in the sink. The fridge door was open and the fridge itself empty. It was often empty, given Aunt Glenda's indifference to providing food for her nieces, but tonight there had been a bit of cheese and the remains of a chocolate cake after Aunt Glenda had relented and gone to the shops. Who had taken them? It would take a pretty intelligent and strong rat to open a fridge door. Suddenly a sound came from the hold area.

Harmony went to the hold and opened the door. Here, in the belly of the boat, it was dank and smelly. Harmony shivered and played the beam over coils of rope and over three large packing cases. She approached closer. There was a cloth over each packing case. She was starting to get frightened now. She reached forward and lifted the cloth off the first. It was full of musty old clothes which exploded dust and made Harmony cough and sneeze. When she recovered she lifted the cloth from the second case, which was full of boating equipment: a chain, a rudder, a wet cloth, paint and oil. If there was someone, or something, in here, the third case was the only hiding place left.

Harmony took a deep breath to calm her butterfly heartbeats, then gripped the cloth covering the case – but she never lifted it because at that moment the cloth suddenly lifted itself. There was someone, or something, inside.

Harmony leapt back in terror.

'Aaaagh!' she screamed.

'Aaaagh!' the figure screamed back.

Harmony dropped the torch, which sent mad scrambling beams of light across the hold before the light died as the torch broke. Harmony turned in the darkness to run, but fell over a rope coil.

'Ouch!' she shouted.

'Ouch!' the figure shouted as the crate fell over.

'Who's there? Come on – who is it? I'm armed. I'm trained to kill,' Harmony warned, but the figure in the dark was having problems of its own.

'Blast and bovril! Stupid nerky twit-faced dink!'

'Who is that?' Harmony asked, curiosity starting to calm her fear.

'No one. There's no one here, so get out of it! Buzz off! I've got a baseball bat and I'll brain you if you don't,' the figure said.

Harmony switched on a light. Standing before her was a scowling, grubby-faced person, possibly a girl, wearing a woolly hat and with the remains of chocolate cake around her chops.

'You must be the bad speller who scrawled the message in the window, and the one who nicked the cake,' Harmony said.

The stranger scowled again.

'Not me. Now stuff off and leave me alone, you sad loser,' she said.

'You don't seem to realize that this is my auntie's boat, and you're the intruder,' Harmony said.

'I was here first. I'll fight you for it.' This odd little person was starting to intrigue Harmony. It was something about the mixture of fear and ferocity in her eyes, her cheek and the fact that she was a mystery.

The noise had awoken Aunt Glenda, who now approached the hold in her dressing-gown, constable's hat and wielding a monkey wrench.

'Harmony, is that you?' Glenda asked.

Harmony looked at the stranger and in that moment a silent pact was made. Harmony wouldn't turn her in, at least not until she found out who she was.

'Yes, it's me. I thought I heard a noise, but it's no one. Go back to bed,' Harmony said.

With a grumble and a sigh Aunt Glenda trundled back to bed.

Harmony stared at the stranger and she stared back.

'You can stay. Just for tonight. What's your name?' Harmony asked.

'Eric,' said the girl.

'But you're a girl, aren't you? What's Eric short for?'

'Dorothy,' said the girl.

She was clearly nuts, and Harmony was tired. Further questions would have to wait until tomorrow. She let the girl settle down in the hold, where she fell instantly asleep, then went back to her own bed.

The next morning was frantic. Puddle decided to harass Melody and followed her everywhere, staring deeply and unblinkingly at her until Melody thought she would go mad.

'This oversized budgie has to go. I think she's got some sort of mental problem,' Melody said, backing away as Puddle advanced.

'So have you, but we keep you,' Harmony countered.

There was also the problem of the plants. Melody and Harmony's father had left all his beloved plants with the girls, and they flourished on the deck of the boat. Now Aunt Glenda had said they had to go. And quick. What were they to do with over fifty large plants? Despite the hassle, Harmony's thoughts were with the strange little girl. She even began to wonder if she had dreamed the whole episode. Eventually Aunt Glenda went off to work and Melody went to do her stint in the café where she worked for a few hours every day.

Harmony took some toast and cornflakes down to the hold, where the girl grabbed the lot and wolfed it all down as if she hadn't eaten for a week.

'Quite an appetite for a midget, haven't you?' Harmony said. 'Will you tell me your name now?'

'Hitler,' the girl said.

'Very funny. I need to call you something.'

'Then call me a cab,' the girl said, finishing the last of the cornflakes.

Harmony's patience, never great, was getting thinner.

'Look, all I have to do is tell Aunt Glenda and she'll get her police friends, then you will be in big trouble,' Harmony said.

The girl's jaw dropped and suddenly she looked small and frightened.

'No police. Please. No police. I'll tell you things,' the girl said.

Harmony had obviously touched a raw spot.

'OK. First – do you know anything about that weird sudden thunder and shaking?'

The girl smiled. 'It was dead cool. Every time I wished you'd all get lost, the boat sort of shook and shimmered,' she said.

This was worrying. Someone whose wishes could cause havoc. What else could she do?

The girl told Harmony that she had been on the boat for several weeks. When there had only been Glenda there, it was fine because she went to work so the girl could have the place to herself during the day. Then Harmony and Melody arrived and that made life more difficult. She took a large biscuit tin from beneath a cloth and opened it.

'This is for my special things. I've never shown anyone else. Not ever,' she said.

She showed Harmony a few articles: a book, a magnifying glass, some postcards and a few coins. One of the coins was a fifty-pence piece. Harmony stared at it. And she knew.

'What's up?' the girl asked.

'Oh boy. Life is full of surprises,' Harmony said, picking up the coin, which glinted in a shaft of light. There could be no mistake. Harmony knew. 'Let me introduce you to the Queen's Nose,' she said.

What happened next showed that the Queen's Nose had lost none of its power.

CHAPTER 2

'Yeah, yeah, sure it is. This coin can make wishes come true, and camels can fly and there's fairies living in my armpits. You are seriously short of onions,' the girl said after Harmony had explained how the Queen's Nose worked.

This infuriated Harmony. She was even more infuriated when the girl refused to give her the coin, so she decided to teach her a lesson, or at least let the coin do so.

'Test it then. Go on. I dare you,' Harmony said.

The girl's eyes narrowed. 'How?' she asked.

'Well, you're a bit of a liar, so wish that every time you tell a lie the Queen's Nose will give some sort of sign. Go on. I dare you,' Harmony said.

'That's stupid,' the girl scoffed.

'You're scared,' Harmony scoffed back.

That did it. The girl grabbed the coin, closed her eyes tightly and rubbed the Queen's Nose just as Harmony had told her to do.

'I wish that every time I tell a lie you will give a sign, o mighty coin, ha ha ha.' She opened her eyes and looked triumphantly at Harmony.

'See? Zero. None out of ten for the Queen's conk.'

'You'll see,' said Harmony. 'What's your name?'

'Donald Duck,' said the girl.

Nothing happened.

'Where did you come from?' Harmony asked.

'The toilet,' said the girl.

Nothing happened.

'Who are your parents?'

'Minnie and Mickey Mouse,' the girl replied.

Something happened.

The girl started to grin triumphantly at Harmony, then she closed her mouth abruptly and her cheeks started to swell. Harmony thought the girl was going to be sick, and she stepped back out of range. The girl's face grew red, then purple, as if her head was about to burst like a squashed grape. With a great whoosh of air she opened her mouth and out lolloped her tongue – if indeed it was her tongue. Harmony thought it looked more like a lizard's, for it was now about ten centimetres long and hung down over her chin like a rubbery bookmark. This was extremely interesting.

The girl was horrified at having this long alien tongue to manage. She rolled it back with her fingers but it seemed to be too big for her mouth and lolled out again with a spring and a slurp. She tried again to push it back in her mouth.

Harmony was entranced. This was the most interesting thing that had happened since Melody had to be freed by the fire brigade after Harmony put superglue on the toilet seat.

'Wicked! Do it again,' she said.

'Like h . . . lllll,' the girl started to say, but opening her mouth merely allowed the tongue to escape again. It hung down like a living tie. Harmony would have liked to examine it more closely, but Melody called her from up on deck. Harmony wasn't quite ready to introduce this new person to her sister, or to Aunt Glenda, so she went to see what Melody wanted.

Melody was surveying Mr Parker's plants. Aunt Glenda had give an ultimatum – either they found somewhere else for the plants by that evening or the lot were going into the canal. They took up a lot of space. What could they do with them?

'Sell them?' Melody suggested.

For once she had had a reasonable idea. Maybe there was a brain of sorts lurking in that skull somewhere, Harmony thought. The girls could have a stall at the Community Centre near the café where Melody worked. It would be a start for the Garden Centre Mr Parker dreamed of starting when he returned.

They stacked a wheelbarrow high with plants, and Harmony wheeled it along the canal towpath to the Community Centre while Melody started to sort out the rest of the plants.

'You need a man to do all that stuff. I could do all your lifting and you could mend the holes in my vest,' someone behind her said. The voice had all the music of a piece of lead piping. Melody turned to face Gus and his pet pig, Grunter. Gus was not a pleasant sight. He rarely washed and had pinkish nostrils from constant nose picking. The only activities around the area of his brain were the scuttlings of head lice through his unwashed hair. He was holding a jam jar of flies which he intended to let die, very slowly. A few of them buzzed feebly against the glass.

'I need you like I need a hole in the head,' Melody said.

Gus frowned. 'Why do you need a hole in the head?' he asked, seriously bemused.

'Just go away and squeeze your blackheads or something. I have a lot on my mind,' Melody snapped, knowing that all insults passed through the space in Gus's head and never lingered for more than a moment.

'What's on your mind, then?' Gus asked.

'Work and life and me and philosophy. Not that you'd understand philosophy,' Melody said.

She was right. Gus had never even heard the word before, but Grunter, who was an exceptionally intelligent pig, knew precisely what Melody meant, and he answered her: 'Grunt gruntle!' which is what she heard, but which, translated, means 'I'm pink therefore I'm spam'. It was a mystery to Grunter that he should have such profound thoughts but that when he tried to communicate them all that came out was 'Grunt gruntle'.

Life was far from fair, he thought, as Gus continued his unsuccessful attempt to woo Melody.

'D'ya wanna come round for dinner? We's having sausage and spuds with brown sauce. Grunter's having a load of dodgy meat-pies me dad found on the road.'

'Grunt gruntle [translation: I can hardly wait,' said Grunter.

Harmony returned and made a fuss of Grunter, which he liked, then the two girls loaded up some more plants and took them to the Community Centre, Gus watching Melody walk away with an ache in his heart which could have been unrequited love, but was more likely to be caused by the three tins of cold beans he'd wolfed down for lunch, the remains of which were still drying on the front of his T-shirt.

Harmony had decided to let the stranger in the hold stew in her own misery for a few hours, so that she could gain a proper respect for the power of the Queen's Nose.

She waited until supper was over, then put some food in her pockets.

'What are you doing?' Aunt Glenda asked.

'There's a mad strange child in the hold with a tongue half a metre long. I'm taking her some supper.'

Harmony knew no one would believe her, and she was right. It was strange how the truth was often so unbelievable. She gave a few scraps to Puddle, who was just working up to a happy evening tyrannizing Melody, then went to the hold, pocketing her camera on the way.

The girl wasn't there. Harmony looked around, then she noticed that the skylight was open. She climbed on a coil of rope and scrambled up through the skylight to where the girl was sitting on deck, looking down at the oily swirls of the canal. She was a perfect picture of misery. Harmony approached, smiling, and gave the girl some bread, fruit and cheese. The girl took the food and opened her mouth but her tongue lolled out. She tried curling it around an apple, then she tried holding her tongue to one side, but somehow it always managed to get in the way.

'Highly curious,' Harmony said. 'Want to try telling the truth?'

'I am tellllllling the tlllllluth . . .' the girl spluttered, her tongue immediately growing another half-metre. Now it flopped down as far as her waist. Most people would have found it disgusting, but Harmony thought it was one of the coolest things she had ever seen.

She took out her camera and photographed the girl. 'For scientific purposes,' Harmony said.

This made it worse. The girl looked even more miserable and then, try as she might to hide them, tears tumbled down her cheeks and splashed in great wet drops on the deck.

Harmony's feelings softened. 'Look – the coin's

telling you to cool it with the lies. At least don't lie to me. The coin knows me,' Harmony said.

'What shall I dllllloooo?' the girl dribbled as her long tongue flopped and curled down her chest to her waist.

'Tell me your name,' Harmony said.

'My real name's . . . Gelllalldine,' the girl spluttered, feeling sick every time she tried to speak.

'Gelatin?' Harmony asked.

'Gelllalldine!' the girl said miserably.

'General Dean?' Harmony asked.

'Gelllalldine! Gellalldine! Are you dlleaf?!'

'Ah. Geraldine,' Harmony said, understanding at last.

'Yeah, but don't you dare call me thlllat or I'llll plunch your flace in. Call me . . . Dllll, Dino!' the girl said with a great effort.

'Dino. I like it. Hi, Dino,' Harmony said, holding out her hand for a Yo handshake.

Dino responded.

'How long have you been here?' Harmony asked.

' 'Bout two months. Hey! It's getting smaller!' Sure enough, the long and ridiculous tongue was starting to coil back and shrink.

'The Queen's Nose. It's had its fun. How old are you?' Harmony asked.

'Elll . . . eb . . . eleven,' Dino said. With a huge suck-ing slurp the tongue shrank even more, and as Dino poked it out it was almost back to normal. She looked down at the tip of it, going cross-eyed, then she opened her special tin and took out a small pocket mirror to examine her tongue properly. In the tin was a book with the words 'The Queen's Nose' on the cover. Harmony stared at it.

'You didn't tell me about this,' she said.

'You didn't ask,' Dino replied. 'Anyway, it's rubbish. The book's stuck closed. I've tried everything to get it open, even a chisel.'

Harmony took the book and, to the surprise of both of them, the book fell open, the pages fluttering like leaves in a breeze, eventually stopping at a page which had a picture of a snowstorm, tiny snowflakes falling from the top to the bottom of the page.

The snow cleared and Uncle Ginger's face appeared. He smiled.

'Uncle Ginger, it's you! Cool. And the Queen's Nose is back. I can't wait to start wishing,' Harmony said.

'Ah, but you can't, Harmony. Only Dino can wish now – under your guidance, of course,' Uncle Ginger said.

Harmony felt outraged. 'But why? You gave the coin to me! It's not fair,' she said.

'The concept of fairness is wishful thinking,' Ginger said. 'The coin has a purpose – you can be sure of that. *Au revoir*,' and he was gone.

Harmony was annoyed that she couldn't wish, but she had to admit to herself that things were starting to get interesting on the boat, and Dino was intriguing.

Where did she come from? Why was she there? Where was her family? Why did she sometimes have a haunted look in her eyes? Why was she terrified of the police? Harmony knew that Dino would just clam up if she was bombarded with questions, so for now, and much against her impetuous nature, Harmony decided to be a bit patient. If she had known what was going to happen that night, however, she wouldn't have let Dino out of her sight.

She did have another major problem on her mind, though: Puddle had mysteriously disappeared. Usually the most punctual of ducks when it came to appearing at mealtimes, Puddle had missed supper, so Harmony decided to go looking along the towpath for her. She told Dino to go back down to the hold and in the morning she would introduce her to Melody and Aunt Glenda.

Dino sat for a long time in the hold, holding her tin and looking at a spider that was tirelessly weaving a magnificent web in a corner. Then, when it was quite dark, she got up and left the hold. As she did so a shadow appeared on the wall, but not hers. The shadow was of someone wearing a long coat and a fedora hat. The shadow stood very still and appeared to be watching Dino depart.

A few minutes later Dino was in Harmony and Melody's room. She was wearing a balaclava to hide her

face. She went straight to a small dressing-table a
opened Melody's jewellery box. Bangles, earrings and
necklaces glittered there. Dino stared at them for a
moment, then started to stuff them into her pockets. A
slight sound made her turn. She thought she glimpsed
a shadow that flickered and disappeared as she turned.
As it did so, Melody appeared, about to enter. Melody
saw Dino at once and she pulled up sharply. Quickly
Melody slammed the door shut from the outside and
locked it, and then she screamed 'Help!'

Aunt Glenda appeared in her nightie and curlers, brandishing a cosh with 'HEADBANGER' printed on it.

'What's wrong? Who's there?' she asked.

'A burglar, an intruder – in there!' Melody said.

'Stand back!' Aunt Glenda said, puffing out her chest and throwing herself at the door, which shattered into a hundred pieces, and Aunt Glenda went sprawling across the room.

'Why did you do that? I've got the key,' Melody said.

'One should always have a proper sense of drama on these occasions,' Aunt Glenda declared, rubbing her knee where it had cracked on the edge of the bed. The room was empty. They looked under the bed and in the wardrobe, but a fluttering curtain made it clear that Dino – although neither of them knew who it was, of course – had escaped through the window. Melody held up her empty jewellery box and harboured dark thoughts about hanging, quartering, boiling and mincing jewel thieves.

Meanwhile Dino had sprinted along the towpath and hopped over a fence and now was running across some waste ground, clutching her tin and feeling the weight of the jewellery in her pockets. She had no idea she was being followed until Harmony rugby-tackled her from behind and they both landed with a *whumph!* on the ground. Harmony had seen Dino running along the towpath and had given chase.

'What are you doing?' Dino asked. 'You could have broken my legs and then I'd have nothing to kick you with.'

'The question is: what are *you* doing? I told you to stay hidden until tomorrow,' Harmony said.

'I'm a free spirit. I needed air. I came out for a jog,' Dino lied.

'Do you always take my sister's jewellery out for a jog?' Harmony asked, looking down at a necklace which had fallen out of Dino's pocket.

Dino said she panicked, took the jewellery and ran, that she began to think that Harmony had gone for the police, that she couldn't trust anyone. She said there were things she would tell Harmony about herself, but not now. She begged for another chance and, although she didn't really know why, Harmony decided to give her one. She took the jewellery back to the boat and gave it to a surprised Melody, saying that a man had dropped the things on the towpath as he ran away.

Melody didn't believe Harmony, but at least she had her jewellery back.

An hour later a tired Dino crept on to the boat and fell asleep in the hold. Tomorrow she would meet Melody properly, as herself and not as a thief.

Harmony lay on her bed, wondering who this odd girl was. Clearly she wasn't to be trusted, but Harmony had a hunch that for the moment she should be indulged. It was almost as if she knew her, even though they had only just met.

'There's a grubby-faced dwarf at our table,' said Melody, eyeing Dino suspiciously.

Dino gave a wide grin and started to hoover down her fourth bowl of cornflakes.

'Meet Dino,' Harmony said.

Aunt Glenda eyed this new child suspiciously. Both she and Melody assumed that this was a friend of Harmony's who was just visiting for breakfast.

'Why is he eating so much?' Glenda asked, thinking Dino was a boy.

''Cos she's hungry,' Harmony said. 'More importantly, has anyone seen Puddle?'

No one had. It was very worrying. A suspicion began to form in Harmony's mind that perhaps Dino knew something about Puddle's disappearance. She would keep an eye on her. It also transpired that some money had been taken from the boat and despite Dino pleading with her eyes that it wasn't her, it seemed pretty obvious to Harmony that it was. She'd sort that out later.

Now she had to go and meet Gregory at the plant stall. She and Melody had made a start on it, but it looked a bit pathetic, so Harmony had telephoned Gregory, Melody's old boyfriend, and had asked him to come and help kickstart the business for them, given that although he was often a dope in life he had a good brain for business.

Gregory looked at the little wooden stall and sighed. It was going to be a long job. He decided on ways of raising money to buy more things, how to expand the range of things to sell, and he bullied a few local pensioners who were sitting in the café to come and help out as unpaid assistants. While he busied himself with all that, Harmony took Dino aside.

'Right. I want straight answers from you. Did you take the money from the boat?' Harmony asked.

'No!' Dino replied.

'Do you know where Puddle is?'

'No! And stuff you for thinking I do know!' Dino said, turning on her heel and walking away.

There was one person who knew exactly what had happened to Puddle. In fact he was looking at her at the same moment that Dino turned her back on Harmony.

Gus was in his shed, in the yard near the caravan where he lived with his dad. The shed was dirty and smelly, full of piles of old newspapers, empty tins, oil cans and old bits of machinery which Gus had converted to make miniature torture machines for insects. Gus sat on a crate scooping beans out of a tin with his grubby fingers. He belched loudly. Grunter watched Gus and Gus looked at Puddle, who was in a wooden box with mesh over the top to prevent her escaping.

Gus leaned closer to Puddle, who spat defiantly up at him. Gus grinned.

'Orange sauce. That's what you have with duck. We'll have brown sauce though. And a big pickled onion stuffed in your gob. Gotta be nice and fat though. Like some beans?' Gus said.

He turned to Grunter.

'This'll show Harmony she ain't so clever. And you better not tell her, Grunts, otherwise you're sausages.'

And Grunter, who wanted to live as long as possible, said: 'Grunt gruntle grunt,' which means, 'My lips are superglued, brother.'

As Gus left his shed, followed by Grunter, Dino was returning to the boat. She looked at Gus and wondered.

Gregory now referred to the plant stall as the Garden Centre, and things were moving fast. He had bought hundreds of pounds' worth of new plants. When Harmony asked where he had got the money, he said it was a loan and he had used the boat as collateral, which meant that if things went wrong with the Garden Centre and it made no money, then Aunt Glenda lost the boat.

Harmony decided it would be best not to tell Aunt Glenda about this new development. Besides, her attention was currently occupied by Melody, who had taken her to one side and was obviously furious with her, though Harmony didn't have a clue why.

'You're trying to make a fool of me by making up to Gregory!' Melody spat.

So that was it, Harmony thought. Melody seriously thought that she was interested in Gregory as a . . . boyfriend! Ha! Melody was jealous.

Harmony laughed, which made her sister more furious.

'What's the big deal? If you don't fancy him any more, why get in such a state?' Harmony asked.

'You obviously have no understanding of emotions. I may not want him but I don't want him to fancy anyone else. I don't want him back but I want him to want me to want him back and although I don't think of him as someone I fancy I do think about him as someone whom I want to fancy me still, so in that sense I do think about him. Without thinking about him. Do you see?' Melody said, breathless and agitated.

'I'm leaving now. I suggest you lie down in a dark room in the hope that a brain may grow,' Harmony said, and left Melody to wander in the strange minefield that people call 'relationships'. Give me friendships with animals any time, Harmony thought.

★   ★   ★

The afternoon brought disaster. With the help of his pensioner army Gregory had erected a large gazebo with stalls inside. There was also a greenhouse for the plants, now numbering several hundred, and Gregory had given them all a strong spray of powerful fertilizer. That was his first mistake. The instructions stated: USE SPARINGLY. OVERUSE MAY DAMAGE PLANTS. Gregory hadn't read this crucial bit of information. Neither had he realized that while plants like light, they didn't like being microwaved, so turning up the heater to full had been his second mistake, and it explained why most of the plants had third degree burns and needed emergency surgery.

Harmony and Gregory looked at the steaming, choked plants.

'I think we need a bit of assistance. Something special,' Harmony said.

Back on the boat, Dino took some persuading. Harmony told Dino that she (Harmony) believed that she (Dino) regretted taking the jewels and that she (Dino) didn't take the money. She (Harmony) was also starting to doubt that she (Dino) had had anything to do with Puddle's disappearance. Why would she take Puddle? It made no sense. Finally, after much flattery, persuasion and the loan of a pound, Dino agreed to use the Queen's Nose. She took it out of her tin, rubbed the nose and wished.

'I wish that the Garden Centre business will grow and grow,' she said.

'Thanks,' said Harmony.

As Harmony walked back to the Garden Centre, she decided that if Puddle hadn't returned by the evening she would go to the police and the RSPCA, she would leaflet the area and, if all else failed, she would persuade or bully Dino into using another wish to find Puddle.

The Queen's Nose had already been busy, as Harmony discovered when she arrived at the Garden Centre. It was one of the most extraordinary sights she had ever seen. Gregory was standing just outside the greenhouse, staring inside, his mouth agape and his eyes wide.

'I do not believe this,' he said as Harmony approached. He stepped inside and a large plant tendril knocked him sprawling.

'Amazing. Spectacular. Cool. Little Shop of Horrors, eat your heart out,' Harmony said when she saw what had happened.

Slowly they both entered.

The greenhouse was full of plants in tropical abundance and of ridiculous proportions. Rubber plants had leaves the size of washbasins, creepers were growing and sprouting and coiling and twisting while you watched. One plant had leaves which looked like large, moist lips, another had swivelling eyes on stalks. A row of tiny conifers were singing like a celestial choir: 'Alleluia! Alleluia!' and a plant with strange tartan leaves and a scowling plant face in the centre was muttering Scottish obscenities: 'Haway ye scanny bags 'n' grit yr greeps or I'll spit on yr sassenach heeds 'n' nach the noo my bonny bumbeegs!' It was a whole world in itself, ever changing shape, shifting, expanding.

Melody arrived and the large-lipped plant immediately grabbed her with its tendrils and tried to kiss her.

'Aaghhh! Get it off!' she screamed.

Gregory and Harmony managed to pull her away from the clutches of the plant.

Melody wiped her lips frantically with a tissue. 'Ugh! Obscene. I'm probably diseased!' she said.

'So's the plant now it's snogged you,' Harmony said.

'I'm never going to come to this stupid place again. And I want that plant thing arrested and shot and hung and chopped up,' Melody said, then she left, an obese geranium belching in her face as she did so.

Gregory's brain had moved into overdrive. Where Melody saw horror and humiliation he saw potential, publicity and profit. This wasn't a Garden Centre. It was a miniature theme park, and these plants would have the crowds fighting to get in for a look. Whatever had caused this had done them a very good turn.

When Aunt Glenda arrived home from work she decided to stroll along to the Garden Centre to see how things were progressing. She imagined that the girls and Gregory might have sold a few plants, but she was not at all prepared for what she did see. It was amazing just how quickly word had got round about the strange things growing at the Garden Centre. A queue had formed all the way round the Community Centre and snaked towards the Garden Centre, which now had a big hand-painted sign proclaiming it as GREEN FINGERS THEME PARK – ENTRANCE £2.50. She pushed her way to the front and looked at the plants. The kissing plant was trying to give great wet smackers to everyone near it. The choral conifers were singing their little green hearts out: 'It's good to touch the green green grass of ho-me, oh yeah!' The Scottish plant had become so fierce, spitting phlegm and acrimony at everyone, that a coil of barbed wire had been placed around him.

'Are these things real?' Aunt Glenda asked.

'As real as this,' Gregory said, opening a cash box full of coins. 'Er, by the way, that'll be two pounds fifty, please.'

A short distance away, dark and secret things were happening that had more to do with pain than profit. Gus was in his shed, his once white T-shirt stained with dribble and bean juice. He was sharpening an axe on a stone. The steel edge squeaked horribly and started to gleam as the new sharp edge was laid bare. Grunter stood in the corner, watching impassively. Puddle stared from her box, her brilliant dark eyes defiant, even though she sensed exactly who that axe was being sharpened for.

Gus turned and looked at her. 'I reckons you're fat enough anyway. Like a roly poly Christmas pud. Plenty of meat. Be a nice surprise for Dad. Duck and chips. Might even offer a bit to that Harmony – then tell her who she's just eaten. Come on, Quackers, show us that nice juicy neck.' He reached down towards Puddle and lifted the wire from the box.

Puddle opened her beak and gave him a good strong nip. He drew back in pain.

'Right! Bite me, would you, eh? I was only going to kill you and eat you. But now I'm gonna torture you as well.'

Grunter looked horrified. Today the duck, tomorrow the pig perhaps? He grunted several times, which meant, 'For the record, I want everyone to know I am against this.'

Gus grabbed Puddle and yanked her out of the box. She started to choke as he squeezed, her wings flapping and her feet pedalling in panic. Blood was oozing from Gus's hand where Puddle had bitten him, and a few drops splashed on her feathers.

Outside, a few hundred metres away, a small figure was sitting hunched, by the towpath. Dino had been watching the shed for an hour now, brooding and feeling that the world was often against such as she. How could Harmony think that she'd hurt Puddle? And what was Gus up to in that shed?

CHAPTER 4

Something told her it was time to act. Dino approached the shed and stood about thirty metres away from it, in the scrapyard. If Gus came out for her she knew she could run faster than him, but it was still wise to give herself a head start. She thought she could hear something going on inside – a squawk? A grunt? What?

'Gus! Gus Grobbler! I want a word with you!' she shouted. 'Come out of that smelly shed!'

This shed smells? Grunter thought. Somehow, he had always thought of it as a pleasant pong of sweat and dirt and muck. Oh well, no accounting for taste. Gus held on to Puddle and listened.

Dino's voice carried across the scrapyard as she shouted louder. 'I know you've got Puddle. And I'm going to punish you, Grobbleguts. You are going to pay! I'm going to make it so that even the worstest smelliest bellysmeller bugfaced vomithead will be better off than you. You are as ugly as you are thick!'

Now, you might think that this was a mistake, given that Gus was bigger than Dino, and if he did catch her she might well have got something broken, but, as Dino knew, Gus was not a subtle thinker, and his attention was best caught by loud simple words.

She was right, because Gus put Puddle down and opened the shed door. 'When I get hold of you you're dead,' Gus said, stretching his verbal wit to its extremities.

'When I get hold of you you're dead,' Dino mimicked him in a thick mocking voice. 'Gus, what's the difference between your head and a grapefruit? A grapefruit thinks more. I know you've got Puddle. Give her back.'

Gus sneered, went back inside the shed and slammed the door.

Dino took the Queen's nose out of her pocket, rubbed the nose and wished as hard as she could.

'I wish, I wish that something will happen to make Gus pusface Grobbleguts well sorry he took Puddle.' Then she settled down to wait.

It didn't take long. A few minutes later, the shed door opened and Gus backed out then ran to the Grobbler caravan, followed by a squeaking Grunter.

Dino ran into the shed and scooped up a terrified but otherwise unharmed Puddle. Now Harmony would know Dino was on her side, even though there were things she couldn't tell her. Not yet anyway.

Dino carried Puddle out of the scrapyard and along the towpath, unaware that on the other side of the canal, standing behind a tree like a snake watching a rabbit, was a tall figure in a long coat. He spent a lot of time watching Dino, but he wasn't ready to make his move. Not yet.

Dino carried Puddle to the Garden Centre, and Harmony was ecstatic. She gave Puddle a big kiss on the beak and stroked her feathers.

'Thanks, Dino.'

'Think nothing of it,' Dino said.

It was clear to Harmony that Dino was making a real effort to please, and she began to think that perhaps this girl would become a real friend.

'Where was Puddle?'

'Gus had her.'

'Little toerag,' Harmony said. 'Execution would be too good for him.'

'Yeah! That's why I . . .' Dino began.

'That's why you what?' Harmony asked, eyeing Dino suspiciously.

'Nothing. Nothing at all,' Dino said.

There were times when it was best to say nothing and just let events speak for themselves.

Events were about to speak very loudly to Mr Grobbler. He'd had a hard day trying to sell some scrap iron back to the railway company he had stolen it from a few months before. Now he had his feet up in the little ramshackle dirty caravan he and Gus called home. On his lap was a large plate swimming with eggs, tomatoes, gravy, ketchup, chips, peas, beans and something that might have once been a sausage. He was watching an old Hollywood movie on TV, about a little girl who had lost her pony, and a tear ran down his cheek. Then he heard Gus.

'Dad. Dad. Look.'

And when Mr Grobbler turned around his mouth fell open and the sausage fell off his fork.

What he saw was Gus, but a much changed Gus. Mr Grobbler had always looked at his son with eyes so favourably prejudiced that he actually believed Gus to be good-looking and intelligent, rather than the inflated and snotty baggage other people saw, but even Mr Grobbler was shocked now. All Gus's hair had fallen out and his face, never his best feature anyway, was covered in large medieval-looking boils and hairy warts. He was a picture of repugnance and looked like an advertisement for fatal skin diseases.

'My boy! My one and only! What's happened to you? Your golden curls vanished. Your velvety skin gone.'

'It's all over. Look,' Gus said, taking off his shirt to reveal a torso covered in pustular boils, brown warts and hairy pimples.

'Does it look bad, Dad?' Gus asked.

'What? No, no, my boy. Just a few teenage spots. You're just as handsome as ever,' Mr Grobbler said, not wishing to alarm Gus even more.

But when Gus walked over to a mirror he found therein the truth. He gazed at himself. He examined the wreckage of his face and the ruin of his body, and he smiled. Yes, smiled. Because in the ugliness he saw a kind of perfection. Somewhere in the dim recesses of Gus's brain he knew he wasn't good-looking or even remotely attractive; if that was the case, then how much better to be ugly and, best of all, to be the ugliest and most disgusting person of all. There was a kind of distinction in it, a purity. Now people would know he was around all right. Such were the strange ley-lines of his thoughts as he stared at the weeping mess of his face and body.

'I look horrible! Brilliant! Look at them big 'uns. Ha ha. Now people will take notice of Gus Grobbler. I can get the best seats at the cinema. Get me own director's box at the football.'

Mr Grobbler was alarmed. Perhaps this awful mutant disease had already destroyed his poor son's mind. 'Gus, my boy, tell me you're joking. No one in their right mind could like it,' he said.

Gus beamed again at his reflection, then he turned and looked seriously at his dad.

'I think it looks wonderful,' he said. 'I could be a famous freak or something. Dad, I've fallen in love with meself.'

'Gus, you can't go around looking like that. I'm taking you to see my old mate Jimmy. You need medical help,' Mr Grobbler said, standing up and putting on his coat.

'Jimmy's a vet, ain't he?' Gus asked.

'Best there is. Specializes in bullocks,' Mr Grobbler said.

The Queen's Nose had been particularly active as a result of Dino's wishes that day. Mr Grobbler hauled Gus off to see Jimmy, who rubbed him with strong horse liniment and told Mr Grobbler to see how he was in the morning.

After taking over three hundred pounds in entrance fees, Harmony and the others were having tea on the boat.

At the Garden Centre, the plants were growing even more and, as dusk fell, they appeared to be murmuring among themselves, like revolutionaries plotting in shadowy corners.

Harmony was excited about the plants and, now that Puddle was back, everything seemed to be going ahead in very satisfactory ways. Getting to know Dino was going to prove very interesting, she thought. There were mysteries to be solved concerning her, secrets she was keeping, and Harmony was determined to get to the bottom of them.

'Why do you think the Queen's Nose chose you?' she asked Dino when they were alone together that evening.

'Search me. Maybe because I'm the most intelligent one around here,' Dino said. Her eyes darkened. 'Or maybe . . . because I needed help.'

'What sort of help?' Harmony asked.

Dino was about to say more but then Melody appeared, demanding to know who had taken her deodorant, and the moment was gone. Another time, Harmony thought.

The next morning they were all at the Garden Centre early. A queue had already formed outside, eager to see the strange plants. Overnight, a few new varieties had grown. There was a plant with a set of teeth which was chomping the air and had even taken a few bites out of its own leaves. A cannibal that eats itself – weird, Harmony thought. In fact, all the plants seemed a bit edgy. The sweet-voiced choral plants were now stodgy and thuggish and were chanting football slogans: ''Ere we go 'Ere we go 'Ere we go . . .' It was as if a storm was brewing. The Scottish plant, that Harmony had nicknamed Angry Angus, was in a particularly foul mood and spat at Harmony angrily through the barbed wire surrounding it: 'Haway ye sassenach an' grep yr screed. Howay 'n' grib yr grumbles git an' nach the noo too.'

Gregory appeared not to notice the volatile atmosphere as he looked at his watch. 'Ten seconds to go. Right. We have . . . lift off!'

He opened the doors. There was a rush of people and Harmony took their entrance money as they swarmed in like bees around a honey pot.

That is when it happened.

The plants tried to take over. The choral plants had blown a gasket and were emitting steam over everyone. The kissing plant somehow trapped an elderly gentleman against a wall and was kissing him so hard that he looked as if he might suffocate. Many of the plants had grown tendrils which lashed out and curled around people's ankles and legs, dragging them across the floor.

Angry Angus managed to break through the barbed wire and was shouting in the face of a little girl who was so terrified she burst into tears. 'Hup hup and away ye canny gits an lang may yr lang dreek ye drogy scumbag scrumbog! Haway! My name is Braveplant an' I'll take yous all on if ye don't give us a drink! Hup hup hup!'

People were panicking. Some were also getting hurt as they fell, were pushed, pulled and screamed at by the plants. Gregory tried to reason with Angry Angus, but it was in no mood for listening. Harmony tried to pull the tendrils off people's limbs. Dino tried to rescue the elderly gentleman being kissed to death. Aunt Glenda, who had heard the commotion from afar, arrived and collected some dustbin lids, which she gave to Harmony and Gregory to use as weapons. It was war.

Those who escaped ran screaming from the Centre. The choral plants were manically hissing dry steam and Angus was shouting fit to burst: 'Ach och the noo, I'm parched as a parrot's dossbag!' Melody stood outside, her eyes wide with terror, as Angus tottered towards her on little, green, bandy, stalky legs.

Listening to what the plants were saying, and to judge by their appearance, Harmony suddenly realized what the real problem was: these plants were thirsty. In fact they were so thirsty they'd been driven mad by it.

She turned to Gregory. 'Grogsy, have you actually watered these plants?'

Gregory looked puzzled. 'Well, not actually, not as such, no. I thought they . . . I don't know what I thought.' Gregory might be good with figures, but he was hopeless with plants.

Harmony and Dino fetched water from a rain barrel and started spraying the plants. A grateful hissing noise began, then slowly, slowly, the plants quietened, shrank back, drank in the moisture, and became . . . ordinary plants again.

'Well, I think I handled that rather well,' Aunt Glenda said, ignoring the fact that the inspiration had come from Harmony.

Harmony was about to point this out when Mr Grobbler arrived, accompanied by Gus with a bucket over his head.

'Begging your pardon like, but my Gus is in real trouble and I reckon you lot might know something about it,' Mr Grobbler said.

'Why has he got that stupid bin over his head? Not that I'm complaining,' Melody said.

'I'd leave that where it is if I was you, Missy,' Mr Grobbler said.

But Melody was nothing if not nosy. Before Mr Grobbler could stop her, she yanked the bucket off to reveal Gus in all his frightful new state.

Melody fainted. Everyone else stepped back in horror.

Gus grinned. He had power. He stepped forward and the others stepped back.

Gregory felt nauseous and went to be sick in the toilet.

'You sees my problem,' Mr Grobbler said.

'Blimey. Gross. He's finally mutated,' Harmony said.

'You must get him to a doctor,' Aunt Glenda declared.

'Did better than that. Took him to my mate who specializes in bullocks and horse boils. Covered him in linnyment and whatnot, but it makes no different. Even dear old Grunter won't go near him,' Mr Grobbler said.

'But what makes you think we can help?' Aunt Glenda said.

'He mentioned something about a curse from you lot, then he clammed up,' Mr Grobbler said.

'I can't think what he means. Harmony?' Aunt Glenda asked.

'Search me. Nothing to do with us unless . . .' Harmony looked at Dino.

'Can I be of assistance?' Dino asked, trying to look innocent.

'A word in private,' Harmony said, leading Dino away.

★　　★　　★

'All right. It was me. I used the Queen's Nose. So what? The creep deserves it,' Dino said.

'OK. I agree. But now change him back,' Harmony said.

'What? Waste a wish on that pusbag? Nokey cokey,' Dino said.

'If you don't, he'll have to go to hospital and people will start asking questions. Maybe Aunt Glenda will get her police cronies involved.'

That did the trick, as Harmony knew it would.

Dino put her hand in her pocket, then in the other pocket, then in her back pockets.

'Come on, stop messing about,' Harmony said.

'I'm not. It's gone! The Queen's Nose is gone!' Dino said, her face drained of colour.

CHAPTER 5

It was true. The coin had gone. Unless, of course, Dino was lying again. Harmony had a good nose for sniffing out lies and she believed that Dino was telling the truth. Assuming it hadn't been stolen, the coin must have been dropped somewhere – most likely in the hold where Dino spent much of her time and which was now officially Dino's room, although Aunt Glenda and Melody didn't quite realize it yet. The two girls began a frantic search, rifling through drawers, cupboards, under the bed. Puddle followed them, quacking supportively, but the coin was nowhere to be seen.

Harmony sat down despondently. Puddle quacked once more then gave a particularly rich and loud belch. Harmony and Dino looked at Puddle, then at each other.

'Are you thinking what I'm thinking?' Dino asked.

'Yes,' Harmony said, giving Puddle a serious, inquiring look. Puddle stared back just as seriously. 'Puds, listen carefully. The Queen's Nose. Did you swallow it?'

Puddle opened her beak and gave another window-rattling, rich burp. It served very effectively as a Yes.

'Oh no,' said Harmony.

'So what do we do? Operate?' Dino asked.

Harmony looked alarmed. Puddle looked positively terrified.

'On Puds? No fear. She was only trying to guard the coin, weren't you, Puds?' Harmony said. Puddle quacked in agreement.

'So what do we do?' Dino asked.

'Wait for nature to take its course. Tomorrow morning, I'd say.'

'You're dead cool with animals and birds. You ought to take it up professionally, be a sort of pet counsellor,' Dino said.

Once the idea was planted, it grew in Harmony's mind. A pet counsellor. A pet therapist. Why not? And what began the day as an idea, by evening was a decision, though not a popular one with everybody. Harmony announced to Aunt Glenda at the dinner table that she was going to start her own pet therapy business. Aunt Glenda was looking through some photographs of wanted criminals.

'Not on the boat you're not,' Aunt Glenda said, looking up.

'At the Garden Centre then,' Harmony said.

'I think it's a cool idea,' Dino said, her mouth full of biscuits.

Aunt Glenda turned her attention full on Dino. 'Don't you think it's time you went home, er . . . ?' she asked.

'Dino,' Harmony said.

'Where does he live exactly?' Aunt Glenda asked.

'Quite close by,' Harmony said. 'And he's a she.'

'That boy is a she?' Aunt Glenda said, looking closely at Dino.

'Yes,' Harmony said.

'Very odd,' Aunt Glenda commented, peering at Dino. 'But the point remains, money is tight and I suddenly seem to have turned into a children's charity, against my will. So, Dino, it would be nice if you were gone.'

Rather than being upset by this direct request, Dino took another fistful of biscuits and smiled sweetly at Aunt Glenda.

'You might miss me,' Dino said thoughtfully.

'Try me,' Aunt Glenda replied, returning to her photographs.

Dino nearly choked as she caught sight of one of the photographs. Aunt Glenda didn't notice this, but Harmony did, and was about to say something when Melody entered, slamming doors, in a highly wrought state. Obviously her latest attempt to rekindle Gregory's interest in her had failed, despite the fact that she was wearing a skirt the size of a pocket handkerchief and enough perfume to attract an army.

The next morning, Harmony and Dino were walking slowly behind Puddle along the towpath. Puddle quite enjoyed being the centre of attention and she looked behind her every now and then to make sure the two girls were still following. Then she stopped and wiggled her tail-feathers. Her tummy started to make strange gurgling noises.

'Action stations!' Harmony said. 'We're about to have lift off.'

With a loud PHURT! and a satisfied quack Puddle relieved herself on to the towpath. Harmony and Dino stared down at the copious dollop.

'Well, there it is. Funny old colour,' Dino said.

'Yup. I don't suppose you want to . . . ?'

'Definitely not. She's your duck,' Dino said hurriedly.

So Harmony put on a pair of rubber gloves and rummaged around. Puddle looked on curiously, vaguely surprised that her beloved Harmony was showing so much interest in what she had just produced. Usually people avoided it.

'Eureka!' Harmony announced.

She washed the coin in the canal, then gave it to Dino, who took the coin and, reluctantly, used another wish.

'I wish that Gus will return to normal,' she said, and a short distance away, as Gus was sitting in a hospital room waiting to see a skin specialist, a nurse shrieked and dropped a tray as, before her eyes, Gus's skin heaved and pulled and stretched and healed until he was back to his normal, slightly spotty, ugly self.

Now that that was done, Harmony could concentrate on her new project and hopefully make some serious money from it.

She had made some posters proclaiming: HARMONY PARKER PET THERAPIST, and she spent the rest of the morning pasting them around town. She asked Dino to help but for some reason Dino declined. She said she had other things to do. Harmony decided it was time they had another serious talk so, after putting up her posters, she went down into the hold. Dino had emptied the cupboards of food and now was scoffing a packet of biscuits.

'OK. This morning, when you saw Aunt Glenda's photograph of some criminal, you nearly had kittens. Want to tell me about it?' Harmony asked.

'No,' Dino said.

'Want to tell me anything about you, like what your surname is?'

'No,' Dino said.

'I'm sick of you saying No,' Harmony said.

'Stop asking me dumb questions then,' Dino said.

'You can't expect me to keep covering for you if you won't tell me anything. And look at you scoffing away. You're just a food hoover. A scoff bag. A waste of space.'

'So what do you want me to do?' Dino asked.

'For one thing, you could help out at the Centre a bit more. I'll be doing my pet therapy, and there's some work I was going to do for Gregory. You could do that.'

'What work?' Dino asked suspiciously.

'Not much. Just a bit of . . . shovelling,' Harmony said vaguely.

And so it was that half an hour later Dino found herself at the Garden Centre with a shovel standing in front of a huge pile of steaming dung that needed to be moved, in order to dry out for the plants. Dino was not pleased.

Harmony was extremely pleased because, when she arrived at the Garden Centre, there was a growing queue of people with their problem pets who had come to seek the advice of a therapist. There were some pretty strange cases. The first was a woman carrying her pet flea in a matchbox. She was sure that he, Franco the flea, had become bored and listless. Harmony told her that, for all we know, fleas have very complicated minds and need constant stimulation. She recommended that the woman play classical music to Franco, read him poetry and philosophy and spend quality time engaging him in interesting conversations. She charged the woman one pound fifty for the advice.

Next to come into Harmony's small makeshift office was a boy with an albino hamster.

'This is Ringo. He's got this fear of cats and tries to run away from them,' the boy said.

Harmony looked at little Ringo, at the translucent ruby red of his eyes.

'Don't you think that's a good thing? I mean, he might get eaten if he didn't run away,' Harmony said.

'No. I want him to beat them up. To face 'em out and just beat 'em all up.'

'Right. I think maybe you've got the problem here, not Ringo,' Harmony said, and she made the boy sign a solemn promise that he would not put Ringo's life in danger ever again. She charged him twenty pence.

Outside, a long queue stretched across the car park. Melody was walking across the car park, having decided to tell Gregory that this thing was bigger than both of them and it was silly of him to deny it. She was so engrossed in her thoughts that she didn't even see the queue of pets with their owners until a man approached her and smiled.

'Excuse me, I have to go to the bathroom. Would you look after Herman here for a few minutes, please, and keep my place in the queue? He gets a bit over-affectionate sometimes, so don't let him get carried away.'

With a shock that started in her eyes, travelled to her brain and then invaded every cell in her body Melody realized that the man was holding a very big snake and that this snake was looking at her with what could only be described as great interest. If there was one thing that frightened Melody more than snakes, it was more snakes. She was instantly traumatized into speechlessness and stood, frozen to the spot. The man cheerfully wrapped Herman around her neck and went off in search of a gents loo. Melody stood like a statue, her eyes unblinking and wide, with Herman coiled lovingly around her neck and arms.

Dino was in too much of a bad mood to notice anything. Shovelling the muck was hard, smelly work, and the harder it got the more resentful Dino became. Who do they think they are? she thought. Making me shovel pesky piles of poo around. Why can't *they* do it? Frightened they'll get their lily-white hands all smelly. Oh yes, if it stinks, let Dino do it. And what does she mean – calling me a food hoover? I bet she doesn't know what it's like to be really hungry, and no one to buy food for you. Spoilt brat. She doesn't know anything. Anyway, I can eat what I like, when I like. I've got the Queen's Nose. That Ginger bloke said there were ten wishes and I've already wasted a few. Stuff the rest! I'm going to look after number one.

She threw down the shovel and stomped away, full of thoughts that flashed red and black streaks through her mind. Why shouldn't she use the coin for whatever purpose she wanted? She was the one it had chosen, so it was like her servant and she could have whatever she chose and she didn't have to listen to Harmony Parker or anyone else. People were always saying 'Be careful' or 'Think before you act,' but why should she? Who had ever thought about her, except . . . no, she wasn't going to think about him. Not now, when she didn't have to. Now, she would feed on her anger until there was real grub to be had.

She went back to the boat and searched through the food cupboards. There was nothing but a packet of dried spaghetti. She put it on the table and went down to the hold, took the Queen's Nose from her special tin, rubbed the coin and wished.

'I wish that when I go back to the kitchen that spaghetti will be ready. A great plate of it so that I can stuff myself for as long as I like. All just for me.'

And when she went back to the kitchen, that is exactly what she found. At first.

CHAPTER 6

On the kitchen table, where there had been a packet of dried spaghetti there was now a plate of freshly cooked, steaming spaghetti, with a knife and fork on either side. Dino had eaten spaghetti only once before, so it felt like a real treat to her as she sat down and had great fun twisting the fork round and sucking up the strands. It was delicious. She crammed her mouth full and made great smacking sounds as she chewed and slurped. She was going to eat and eat and eat, and there was no one to say, 'Mind your manners.' Stuff manners! As she ate, Dino imagined a never-ending feast where you never felt full and could just go on eating. Some people want to win the lottery or discover treasure in their garden but, having been hungry too many times in her life, she just wanted to eat.

Food was the last thing on Melody's mind at this moment. In fact, judging from her blank expression it was difficult to know whether she had a mind.

Herman's owner returned and smiled at Melody. 'You two have obviously hit it off. He wasn't too frisky for you, was he?'

Herman was uncoiled from around Melody, but it

made no difference. She stood frozen to the spot, zombie-like, all lights out.

Aunt Glenda arrived on her way home from work and approached Melody. 'Melody? Are you all right?' Clearly Melody was far from all right.

Gregory came over to see what was happening, as did a few other people. Soon, a small crowd of people had gathered around Melody whose eyes were staring, trance-like, ahead of her. Aunt Glenda waved a hand in front of Melody's eyes but there was no response.

'What's up?' Gregory asked.

'Seems to be in some sort of trance,' Aunt Glenda said.

'A short sharp shock should bring her out of it,' an old man suggested.

Gregory filled a bucket full of water from a rain barrel and emptied it over Melody, drenching her but getting no response at all.

'Slap her round the face,' an old lady suggested.

'Blow a whistle loudly in her ear,' someone else suggested.

'Ice cubes down the back.'

'Stamp on her foot.'

'Chuck her in the canal.'

Harmony had finished her therapy sessions and came over to see what was happening. She stared at Melody.

'Comatose,' Aunt Glenda said. 'Appears to be nothing much happening from the neck up.'

'That's normal,' Harmony said.

'People keep suggesting ways to get her out of it, but they're all a bit violent,' Gregory said.

This gave Harmony an idea. She went over to Gus, who was sitting in the dust watching Grunter chew on some plants. 'Gus, do you believe that men should be strong and assertive?' Harmony said.

'I live in a caravan,' Gus said inexplicably.

'I know. Look, let's make this simple. Do you want to kiss Melody?'

Gus's eyes flickered. 'S'pose so.'

'Then do it. She goes for the masterful type.'

Harmony led Gus across to Melody and the crowd parted to let them through. Gus couldn't quite work out what was happening; why suddenly was he being allowed to do something that no one would let him do before? Why did a girl who up to now had put him on a level with elephant dung suddenly want to kiss him? Women were a mystery, as his dad had often told him. Still, if that Melody wanted a plonking great kiss, Gus Grobbler wasn't going to disappoint the poor girl.

The crowd held its breath as Gus approached close to Melody. He wiped his nose on his sleeve, worked up a great deal of phlegm from his throat and spat on the ground, then puckered up his lips and leant forward.

Harmony whispered in Melody's ear: 'Sissie, Gus Grobbler is about to plant a fat wet slobbery kiss right on your lips.'

Melody screamed and came out of her trance. Her eyes started to focus.

'I . . . I . . . I . . . what happened?' she asked.

'You're all right now,' Gregory said.

'I had this feeling someone was going to kiss me. Gregory – you do care!' she said, advancing on him.

'No, no. You've got it all wrong,' Gregory said, backing away. Going out with Melody a few years ago had been like being chained to a lunatic, and he had no intention of repeating the experience.

A job well done, thought Harmony, as she set off back to the boat. If she had known what was happening on the boat she would have run like the wind to get there.

There had been little warning. Dino had just eaten enough spaghetti to fill three adults and six children. Oddly enough, although she ate and ate, there always seemed to be the same amount of spaghetti left on the plate. She stuffed a last forkful into her mouth and pushed the plate away. I am stuffed. Brilliant, she thought. The plate slid back towards her. She pushed it away again. It slid back towards her. She stared at it quizzically, then got up and turned away to get a drink of water. A faint hissing sound made her turn back. The plate now had more spaghetti on it. Dino turned away again. A hiss. She turned back, to see more spaghetti. She looked away and heard another hiss. She turned back, to see spaghetti piled so high that it wobbled on the plate. She stared hard at the spaghetti, which appeared to tire of the cat-and-mouse game and with a vicious hiss started to grow higher while she watched. It was tired of playing and now it meant business.

Dino was suddenly, coldly frightened. She held on to the back of a chair to steady herself.

'What's going on? Stop it!'

The spaghetti was bubbling as if it was alive. She picked up the plate and tipped the lot into the rubbish bin. It started slithering out over the top of the bin, like thin pale snakes. One of the strands coiled around Dino's wrist and tightened.

She yanked her hand free. 'Look, pack it in! It's not funny. I was hungry, that's all.'

She picked up the bin and carried the seething mass to the toilet, emptied the lot down the pan, and flushed it. The spaghetti clearly didn't like this: it hissed and heaved and refused to be flushed. It started climbing up over the toilet seat, so Dino slammed the lid shut and sat on it. The spaghetti pushed angrily then wormed its way along the pipes and started growing and spouting from the cistern above her. Dino had sweat pouring down her face as she backed away and out of the toilet, slamming the door shut behind her. Moments later strands of spaghetti started creeping and hissing under the door, above the door, through the keyhole.

She ran back to the kitchen. A loud hiss from the sink caught her attention. Spaghetti was gurgling and hissing from the plug hole. She felt something tickling, and she looked down to see spaghetti coiling from her shoes and across the floor. Spaghetti coiled from her pockets. She kept thinking to herself, Don't pass out! Don't pass out! because she felt that if she became unconscious the awful stuff would get her. She'd be devoured, buried, stifled. She didn't know what to do, so she opened her mouth and screamed as loudly as she could.

A scream so loud that Harmony heard it all along the towpath. She ran, and two minutes later she arrived at the boat. As she climbed on the deck she stepped on a sea of writhing, wriggling spaghetti. She kicked it away and made her way down to the living quarters.

'Dino? Dino!' she called.

In the kitchen Dino was trying to keep a particularly virulent strand of spaghetti at bay with a long-handled broom. Harmony grabbed a chair and tried to help force the spaghetti back. They talked as they fought back to back.

'Don't blame me,' Dino said, her face hot and flushed.

'You made a wish, didn't you?'

'It's my coin,' Dino said.

A strand of spaghetti looped around Dino's broom and with a hiss pulled it out of her hands.

'We need help!' Harmony said. 'Where's the book?'

'In my room,' Dino said, and they started to fight their way down to the hold. The boat seemed to be filling with spaghetti, and the more the girls fought the more violent it became. One twist was trying to get Harmony in an arm lock. Dino pulled it off and threw it in a corner, where it hissed like a cornered wild animal.

They got to Dino's room in the hold and Dino grabbed her tin from under the bed. She was about to open it when a torrent of spaghetti gushed into the room, knocking Harmony sideways and twisting itself around Dino's legs. As Harmony watched, the hatch at the bottom of the boat opened and the spaghetti started to drag Dino down into the water on which the boat was floating. It didn't make sense, Harmony thought as she struggled to her feet. Water should be pouring into the boat through the hatch, but instead there seemed to be an invisible film stopping it from doing so, but through which Dino was being pulled.

'Help! It's going to drown me!' Dino shouted.

Harmony threw herself across the hold just in time to grab one of Dino's hands, then she tried with all her strength to hold on as the spaghetti tried to pull her down into the muddy brown stew of the canal. Dino's hand started to slip away, then was gone, and with a plop Dino was pulled down into the canal.

'No! No!' Harmony shouted.

'Harmony! Harmony!' someone called.

Harmony looked down, and there was the book open with Uncle Ginger staring up at her from one of the pages.

'Uncle Ginger! You've got to help! Quickly!'

'Always in a rush. How can you think if you're always hurrying?' Uncle Ginger said infuriatingly. How could he be so calm in a life-and-death emergency like this? 'Now, what caused the problem?' he asked.

Harmony stamped on a nasty length of spaghetti that was trying to crush her ankle. 'Dino wished for spaghetti. She's greedy.'

'Right. So let's say greed is a form of selfishness, and maybe only unselfishness can untie knots. Which is where you come in.'

'How?'

'What does spaghetti remind you of?' Ginger asked.

'String. Worms. Knitting. Snakes. Rope,' said Harmony.

'And which could be useful in a rescue?' Ginger asked.

'Rope?'

'Right.'

And Ginger was gone.

In front of Harmony a strand of spaghetti started to

dance like a twirling rope, then it straightened itself and looped down into the water. The end of the rope shook, as if commanding her to take hold of it. She grabbed it and lowered her feet into the water, which was icy cold.

'Here goes nothing,' she said, and slipped down into the darkness.

Harmony held her breath and expected the worst. She knew the canal was horrible, full of muck and waste, and that the only fish to live there would probably be mutants. So she was surprised to see that as the darkness melted she found herself in clear water that seemed to be getting warmer, almost like bath water. She held on to the rope and walked along the bed of the canal, one hand after the other on the rope. Just as she could feel her lungs ache and knew she would need to breathe very soon, the rope turned upwards and she hauled herself up on to the bank of the canal and broke the surface.

She took in a great lungful of air. She was on the other side of the canal, and the rope led through some bushes; she followed it into a clearing where Dino was lying motionless on the ground. The reason she was so still was that she was bound from head to toe in spaghetti like an Egyptian mummy. Despite the horror of all that had recently happened, Harmony couldn't help giggling. Only Dino's flushed and now furious face was visible.

'Just get me out of this. Now!'

The Queen's Nose had shown Dino a thing or two

about greed, and now Harmony was sharing the joke. As she untied Dino neither of them was aware that a third person was watching through binoculars from a field a kilometre away. Someone tall and thin, wearing a long coat.

CHAPTER 7

Melody had had enough. Rejected by Gregory, ridiculed by Harmony as usual, stuck on a rickety old boat all summer with no decent boys around. And now, the morning after the spaghetti incident, the crushing news that she had failed all her GCSEs. Aunt Glenda tried to cheer her up by saying that life was terrible anyway and if you thought you could see a light at the end of the tunnel, it was probably an express train coming straight at you. That didn't help. Dino tried to cheer her up by saying that not many people failed *all* their exams and maybe she would get in the *Guinness Book of Records* as the biggest failure of the 1990s. This did nothing to cheer Melody up either.

She decided to leave home, but she didn't have anywhere to go and, besides, her clothes always got crumpled in suitcases, so she thought she would make a big effort to change her life. She looked through the local paper and among the naff jobs was one interesting one: an Operations Executive at a recording studio, whatever that meant. She applied for it. She also decided that if she was going to have a new job then she should forget Gregory and find a new boyfriend, preferably one who would consider it an honour to spend all his money on her. She put an ad in the personal column of the paper saying that a 'beautiful, sophisticated young lady' wished to meet a 'well-built, rich, sensitive, educated, well-dressed, wildly attractive young guy for expensive evenings out and possible marriage'.

So it was that a few days later, when the paper came out, Melody spent a great deal of time going up on deck to meet potential suitors – young men who thought they might be just the Prince Charming she needed. The first to call was a hip hop dude with long Rasta hair, shades, and every available piece of flesh pierced. His name was Animal.

Melody looked him up and down and wondered what planet he was from.

'Hi. How you hanging, babe? I'm your main man. Name's Animal. You wanna come missin' for some kissin'? Chuggin' for a huggin'? 'Cos I ain't slow, and we can cruise with the news that I'm your number one dude. Gimme a little lip-locker, whaddya say?' he said all in one sing-song rap breath.

'I don't know what you're talking about. Would you go away, please?' Melody said.

'That's cool. Like I'm already gone,' Animal said, and he retreated, still talking to himself. 'I'm so gone I'm nearly comin' back. Hey, if I'm comin' back I might meet myself on the way. How ya' doin', Animal my man? Yo, I'm doin' fine, jus' gettin' my juice together; how's yourself, my man? I'm cool too.'

Melody retreated below deck, away from this danger-ous maniac.

Next was a skinhead called Dennis, whose face, arms and shaven head were covered with tattoos, most of which declared 'I LOVE SHARON'. Then there was a morris-dancer wearing ribbons and bells; then a weedy-looking chap with no front teeth and glasses so thick they made his eyes bug-sized. Last of all was Gus, who stood at the door holding a cauli-flower.

'Yes?' Melody asked, not for a moment thinking that he was there in response to her advertisement.

'I come to answer your wotsit. Ad dubree. To be your boyfriend and snog you. I bought you a cauli-flower. Needs washing a bit. I think there's a caterpillar in it. How about it then?' he said.

Melody felt insulted that Gus could even dream that she might be interested in him.

'I can't believe you've had the cheek to answer my ad. I didn't even know you could read,' she said.

'You ain't up for it then?' Gus asked.

'I'd rather have my head cut off than go out with you,' Melody said.

This seemed pretty definite. Even to Gus.

'So what's wrong with me?' he asked.

'Take a look in a mirror,' Melody said.

Gus stared ahead for a moment, creating the illusion of thought.

'If you don't go out with me I'll blow up your Garden Centre wotsit,' he said eventually.

'You need help,' Melody said as she slammed the door in his face.

Moments later there came another knock at the door. Melody answered it, deciding that there couldn't be that many nerds left in the district. She was pleasantly surprised. Standing there was a very cool-looking young man in jeans and a white T-shirt, with neatly groomed, floppy hair. He was just finishing a call on a mobile phone and had a camera slung around his neck. The moment he saw Melody he took a few snaps of her.

'Sorry. Couldn't resist. I'm a fashion photographer, see, and I was just on the phone to one of my editors, saying that the next time I came across a glamorous girl who could be the next Naomi Campbell I'll just have to shoot.'

Melody was instantly smitten. Good-looking, obviously well off and in a position to make her famous. He seemed just what the doctor ordered. She smiled her widest smile and held out her hand.

'Melody.'

The young man took her hand and kissed it.

'Rod. Rod Strong,' he said.

'Come in, Rod.'

For the next half hour Rod talked a lot about himself while Melody listened. They arranged to meet the next day but one, when Rod would take photographs of Melody.

The following day she couldn't stop talking about how marvellous Rod was and how he was going to make her a star. Harmony had noticed in the past that when someone fancied someone or, even worse, fell in love with them, they became extremely selfish and their brains suddenly seemed to get addled. Harmony hadn't even met Rod and already she was fed up with him.

Melody hung around the Garden Centre all morning, boring Harmony and Gregory to tears. 'After Rod makes me a fashion star I'll be on the front cover of all the glossies and I'll have a yacht in Cannes. Rod says I have near perfect bone structure and an oriental petiteness that sets off my European elegance. He's doing some shots of me tomorrow, did I tell you? But what will I wear? And make-up. I need to practise different styles and looks, but all that foundation plays havoc with my complexion. Harmony, can I practise on you?'

'I wouldn't let you get your claws on me for a million quid,' Harmony said.

'But I must practise on someone. Dino's too ugly and Aunt Glenda's too past it. Who can I use?'

They both looked at Gregory, who glanced up from his accounts book and felt vaguely uneasy. He hadn't been listening to a word Melody was saying, but he didn't like the way the Parker sisters were advancing on him and smiling.

Half an hour later, a protesting Gregory was seated before Melody's dressing-table mirror, appalled at what had been done to him. His hair was spiked up and streaked green so that he looked like a frightened leek. His eyes were heavily made up, but one with blue and the other with pink eye-shadow. Blue lipstick and rouged cheeks added to the overall weirdness.

'Oh no. I'm a freak,' he groaned, horrified.

Harmony and Melody began to assure him that he looked chic and modern when Dino wandered in and screeched with laughter.

'Ha ha! Freak! Freak! The Gobhead from the Green Lagoon.'

'That does it. I'm going home to wash this muck off. See you tomorrow,' Gregory said, and he stalked out with what little dignity he had left.

There was a reason for Harmony helping Melody to practise her make-up. She had heard her sister talking on the phone to a friend, saying that, although she was excited about Rod, she felt dreadful about failing her exams and being unable to get a satisfying job. She felt as if she was a failure. Harmony agreed. But it still nagged at her that her sister was so miserable. She made up her mind to get Dino to use the coin. Despite appeals to her better nature, Dino insisted that her better nature appreciated money as much as her worse nature, so finally Harmony gave her two pounds and Dino wished on the Queen's Nose for Melody to have some success.

As Dino made the wish there was a rumbling and an unsteadying of the boat, as had happened before, and a breeze passed through, ruffling the girls' hair and fluttering open the pages of the Queen's Nose book. The breeze stopped and the book lay open. Writing appeared on the page:

> *You may put M in the frame*
> *but mistakes lead to uncertain gains;*
> *a lark not a peacock may be the way*
> *this wish decides to make matters pay.*

'Brain wobbler,' Dino said.

'M must be Melody. "In the frame." What's that?' Harmony wondered.

'Door. Window. Pictures,' Dino suggested.

'Yes. Photograph. Something to do with old Rodders probably. But I don't get the rest. What do you think, Puddle?'

'Quack!'

The next day Melody got ready by putting on very few clothes and a great deal of make-up. She was dressed to kill. She and Rod were discussing what sort of image she should have in the photographs.

'The inner me,' she said. 'You know, very deep and soulful. A bit of Madonna in *Evita*, all the Spice Girls and something a bit different. The Pope or something.'

Harmony, listening, felt like being sick. How could she have spent two quid on a wish for someone as naff as Melody?

'We need a different background for the shots. Something more natural,' Rod said, flicking back a lock of hair that it had taken ages to get to hang down in the first place.

'How about the Garden Centre plants?' Harmony suggested. 'Melody will blend in well with the creepers.'

So they went to the Garden Centre, where they discovered something very unusual. Sitting miserably at his desk, feebly trying to hide behind a few pot plants, was Gregory, but a much changed Gregory. It was as if he had become a girl. He was wearing make-up, eye-liner and glossy red lipstick, and he had beautiful long blond hair. Harmony tried to pull the wig off, but it wasn't a wig. Then she tried to rub off the make-up, but it was fixed permanently.

'I woke up like it,' Gregory said miserably.

Rod laughed. 'I must get some shots of this!' he said.

'Yes. Let's dress him up!' Melody said, thinking that it would serve Gregory right for not wanting to go out with her again.

So it was that, for the second time in a few days, poor Gregory was manhandled – or, in his current state, girlhandled – to the boat, and forced to dress up despite his protests. They took off his outer clothes and dressed him in a little satin dress, and then Rod took some photographs. Harmony decided that enough was enough and told Melody to give Gregory his trousers back. Instead, she dropped them through an open porthole.

Rod laughed and Gregory turned on him. 'And what are you laughing at?' he asked.

'You. Got a problem with that?' Rod said, still laughing.

'No, but you have,' Gregory replied and, much to everyone's surprise, he punched Rod on the nose.

Rod went down, poleaxed. Melody ran to him. Rod's eyes had crossed, his nose was bleeding and he looked as if all the lights in his head had gone out.

'Oh no. If he's brain damaged he won't be able to make me a star. Gregory, you're a beast,' she said.

'Yes, I am, aren't I? I hit him. Just like that. Pow!' Gregory said, punching the air, ecstatically pleased with himself. This was the first time in his life he had ever whacked someone he didn't like, and it felt good. In fact, it felt wonderful, and he half wished that Rod would stand up so he could knock him down again.

'Nice one, Grogsy. You should wear a frock more often,' Harmony said.

Melody helped Rod off the boat and made him promise to send the photographs of her to his editor first thing in the morning. Then the post arrived with a letter for Melody telling her that she had been offered the position of Operations Executive at Meltdown Recording Studios. She couldn't believe it. Things were really happening for her. She was going to be an Executive in pop music and a top model.

At least, that's what she thought. The Queen's Nose had other ideas.

CHAPTER 8

Melody walked into the Meltdown studio nervously. She had expected a suite of offices with Chesterfield sofas and huge studios with technicians doing mysterious things. Instead, there was one plasterboard room with a few microphones and leads, and a glass partition separating it from the engineer's control room. A figure was hunched over the deck. An oddly familiar figure.

'Hello,' Melody said.

Animal looked up. 'Cool, baby. Like you changed your mind,' he said, assuming that Melody had found him and wanted to go out with him.

'No. I haven't. I'm here for the job. Operations Executive. Er, where is my office and what exactly are my duties?'

Animal roared with laughter. 'Duties? Now I dig that word. Like you're in the army. I mean – chill, my little chickaddy. The name of the game is – be cool. Make honey with the Animal. Hey – I show you your office all right.'

Her office was a dirty little cupboard-sized room with a few brooms and cleaning materials in it. Muck-encrusted coffee cups stood in a filthy sink, and in the corner was one of the worst toilets in the world: it obviously hadn't been flushed in ages. So this was what an Operations Executive was – a cleaner.

Animal beamed and Melody put on a pair of rubber gloves in order to begin her new job. She consoled herself with the thought that once Rod made her a top model she could stop this at once.

Rod Strong was not all he seemed, however. Harmony and Gregory had gone to see a doctor about Gregory's changed condition. The doctor had simply grinned and suggested that Gregory change his name to Marilyn. They were on the bus going back to the Garden Centre, with Harmony assuring the miserable Gregory that something would happen to make him return to normal, when she glanced out of the bus window and there was Rod, dressed in blue overalls, going in through the gates of a factory where toilet rolls were made. So much for the great photographer, she thought.

The next evening Harmony was waiting for Rod when he arrived to see Melody. Dino joined her, ever ready to enjoy watching someone being totally humiliated.

'How does the ad go, Rod? "Jenson's toilet rolls, soft as a baby's doodah". Worked there long, have you?' Harmony asked.

Rod looked uncomfortable. 'I don't know what you're talking about,' he said.

'Oh yes, you do, and if you don't tell Melody, I will,' Harmony said.

A few minutes later Melody came home and kissed Rod. 'When will the photographs be used?' she asked.

Harmony and Dino sat down to enjoy things.

'Over to you, Mister Snappy,' Dino said.

Rod explained that he wasn't actually a professional photographer yet, but that he had sent her pictures off to a top magazine called *Reflections*. He also told her that his name wasn't Rod Strong but Horace Winthrop. He was very sorry if he'd misled Melody and he hoped it wouldn't make any difference to them going out together.

Melody said the only difference it would make was that she never wanted to see his slimebag face ever again, that he was a boil on the backside of humanity, a verruca, a crampfaced codpiece, and she hated him.

Then his mobile phone rang. As he listened his jaw dropped.

When the call had finished he turned to Melody. 'That was Amanda Gladbanger. The editor of *Reflections*. She loves the photographs and wants to do a deal with us. We've cracked it. *Reflections* is one of the biggest magazines in the world. She's coming tomorrow morning.'

'Tomorrow!' Melody shrieked. 'Aagh! Hair! Clothes! Make-up! Action!'

Melody ran off, yelling like a banshee – she had eigh-

teen hours to get dressed and ready. Just enough time
if she hurried. Rod went home to wash his jeans and
put a few professional scuffs on his leather jacket.

That night Harmony sat on her bed with Puddle, puzz-
ling over what had happened and the rhyme she still
didn't understand:

> *You may put M in the frame*
> *but mistakes lead to uncertain gains;*
> *A lark not a peacock may be the way*
> *this wish decides to make matters pay.*

Obviously Melody and the photographs were part of it,
but why had poor old Grogsy turned into a girl? Maybe
it's a mistake, she thought. I'll give it another few days,
and if he doesn't become himself again, I'll cough up a
few more quid to Dino for another wish.

The Queen's Nose had always had a will of its own,
but now that it was in Dino's hands Harmony felt this
was even more the case. There was something uncon-
trolled in the way things happened that sometimes made
her laugh, but occasionally frightened her. And still she
had no idea why the Queen's Nose should have chosen
Dino. Why her? And what was her real story?

The next day Melody was up at four in the morning to
make sure she looked her absolute glamorous best for

the great Amanda Gladbanger. Rod, who still insisted on being called Rod rather than Horace, arrived just after nine and tried to act as cool as an iceberg. He kept looking in a mirror to adjust his hair and practise his smile.

'Do I look all right?' Melody asked.

'Terrible,' Harmony replied.

'Do I look all right?' Rod asked.

'Bit of a plonker,' Harmony said.

Half an hour later, Amanda Gladbanger arrived, doused in a heavy musky perfume and wearing a great deal of leather and jewellery. She breezed in as if she was on show at the Oscar ceremony.

'Hello. You must be Rod,' she said.

'Strong,' he replied.

'I'm sure you are,' she said silkily.

'I'm Melody, and this is my sister Harmony, but I'm afraid they ran out of dress sense by the time they got to her. I am just so thrilled to meet you!' Melody said.

Amanda took some photographs out of a brown envelope and scrutinized them.

'I'll come straight to the point,' she said. 'I'll pay three thousand pounds for a series of shots of the model. This face and figure is just what we're looking for. A sort of hungry and defiant longing. It's different. She could become extremely big.'

'Thank you. I'm just so thrilled,' Melody said. 'What can I say – yes! Yes! Yes! Where do I sign?'

Amanda looked puzzled. 'I'm sorry?' she said.

'The contract? Where's the contract you want me to sign?' Melody said.

'I think there's been some misunderstanding. You are the photographer. Right?' Amanda asked Rod.

'Right.'

'And this is the model we're talking about,' Amanda said. She held up the photographs of Gregory that Rod had taken.

Rod looked dumbstruck. 'Oh no. I forgot. They were on the same roll of film,' he said.

'Gregory!' Harmony said.

'What?' said Gregory, who had just wandered in to do the accounts on the boat because he was fed up with being chatted up by men at the Garden Centre.

Amanda looked relieved when she saw Gregory. 'She's the one! I am going to make you a star, sweetie. Your delicious face and body will be splashed across every magazine from Bangkok to Billericay. You're a mystery. I could eat you. What's your name, sweetie?'

'Gregory.'

Amanda laughed. 'Seriously, is it Marilyn?'

Gregory's face darkened beneath his make-up. 'My name is Gregory and I am a bloke. M.A.L.E. Masculine. Homo sapien. Fellow. Chap. Mister. Monsieur. Señor. Gaffer. Got it?'

Amanda hooted with laughter again. 'A sense of humour too. Just love it. Make that four thousand pounds. You can be our bimbo with brains – it's a great angle.'

Melody was close to tears: all her dreams of stardom were slipping away in this farce. 'I can't bear it, I'm going to work. And I never want to see you again, Horace!' she said, and stormed out.

Amanda told Gregory she could make him/her a millionaire within a year.

Gregory's patience was almost gone. 'I am not your sweetie. I am Gregory. All this hair and stuff is a stupid mistake.'

Rod could see his future disappearing unless he could persuade Gregory to play along. 'No it's not . . . Marilyn,' he said, putting his arm around Gregory, who turned and punched Rod on the nose for a second time. Rod crumpled, unconscious, on the floor. Then Gregory grabbed Amanda's arm and took her outside. Harmony waited, wondering what was going to happen next.

Amanda screamed, and moments later Gregory returned.

'That got rid of her,' he said.

'How did you . . . I mean, what did you show her?' Harmony asked.

'What?' Gregory said. 'Oh, my Arsenal season ticket. Got my name and photograph on it. See?'

Gregory returned to the Garden Centre. Harmony threw a bucket of cold water over Rod, then sent him packing. Melody arrived at work and a miracle happened. At least, she thought it was a miracle. At the studio Animal was supposed to be recording a song with a local boy singer who had got a lucky break – a spot on a television show. However, the girl who was meant to be singing with him failed to turn up for the recording. Melody begged for a chance to sing the female part, and Animal agreed. Much to everyone's surprise, Melody turned out to have a sweet voice, and the song worked. The boy singer asked Melody to join his band. Melody had gone to work a toilet cleaner and she came home a recording artist.

She raced home to tell everyone the good news and found Harmony in the Garden Centre, doing a spot of pet therapy. Harmony suddenly understood the rhyme. A lark is a songbird, and the Queen's Nose had decided that was the way to give Melody success, and not as a flashy model, or peacock. The coin had obviously used Gregory to make sure the modelling didn't work out for Melody. It all fitted and, as usual, the Queen's Nose had chosen a strange way to fulfil the wish.

The sisters left the Garden Centre and started to walk home. They got about fifty metres away when an almighty explosion flung them both to the ground. Great shards of shattered glass flew through the air. Splintered wood, plaster and debris were hurled away like dust being blown. Harmony got to her feet, coughing and spluttering. Her ears hurt from the sound and the shock waves. She looked back at the clearing smoke and the wreckage of the Garden Centre.

'Gregory!' she shouted.

CHAPTER 9

Harmony and Melody ran back to the Garden Centre, Harmony expecting to find Gregory in little bits. The whole place was like a war zone: plumes of smoke, fire, broken glass. She filled a bucket from a rain barrel and threw it against what was left of the door, just as a soot-begrimed figure opened it and emerged.

'Gregory! are you all right?'

'I was until some twit threw water all over me,' he said, coughing and spluttering.

He had been looking for his pen, which had rolled under the desk, and this protected him from the worst of the blast. Also, beneath the scorch marks and the dirt, Gregory had returned to normal. The make-up and blond hair had gone. Harmony assumed it was the shock that did it.

A small crowd gathered, all with their own explanations as to the cause of the explosion: a gas leak . . . faulty wiring . . . plant chemicals . . . aliens . . . Millwall supporters. Aunt Glenda, with her hawk eyes and her nose for trouble, went hunting through the debris, and she found something interesting: an explosive casing, which meant that someone had caused the explosion deliberately. But who?

★   ★   ★

That evening Harmony, Melody, Dino and Aunt Glenda were sitting at the kitchen table.

'Now, has anyone any idea who could have caused that explosion?' Aunt Glenda wanted to know.

Harmony gazed at Dino. Maybe it was someone involved in the mystery that was her past. Maybe it was the man in the photograph she had looked so terrified of. Dino had never explained who he was.

'Don't look at me! Why me?' Dino said. 'I live *here* now, don't I? Why would I want to cause trouble?'

This was news to Aunt Glenda. 'You live here? I thought you were one of Harmony's friends just visiting.'

'It's an extended visit,' Harmony said. Then, anxious to get the subject away from Dino, she said, 'Maybe it was Rod, after Gregory knocked his block off.'

'No. Too much of a weed,' Dino said. 'He'd be worried about getting his shirt dirty.'

'Gus said he was going to blow up the Garden Centre. Maybe it was him,' Melody said, not believing it for a moment. Gus was too brainless to do something like that. Or was he?

They all looked at one another.

'It's no good just suspecting. We need hard evidence,' Aunt Glenda said.

'No. I'm not mixing it up with that psycho again,' Dino said.

★   ★   ★

It was later that evening. Harmony was now convinced it was Gus who had caused the explosion, and she was determined to get proof. For this she needed Dino's help.

'You *are* going to help,' Harmony said.

'How are you going to make me?' Dino asked.

'By offering you money. Three quid,' Harmony replied.

'That's not fair, hitting me in my weak spot. Three pounds fifty,' Dino said.

'Done.'

Gus was in his shed, engaged in some serious maggot breeding. He had a handful of them, and he sniffed at them and watched them as they squirmed and wriggled. He spoke to them softly, in a trance-like voice.

'There. Little babies. You should have seen the explosion. Boooom. Boooom. Beautiful. Magic.'

A knock at the door interrupted his reverie. He opened it. Dino stood there, smiling sweetly. Over Gus's shoulder she noticed a polaroid snap of Melody pinned on the wall with a heart drawn around it in red paint.

Dino spoke so softly and sweetly that it took a while for Gus to register what she was saying. 'Hello, pusface. Do you know? Your ears remind me of garage doors left open. And you're so cross-eyed that when you cry the tears roll down your back. What's up – your brain turned back to the cow poo it was in the first place?'

The insults registered at last. Gus made a grab, but Dino was too nimble, and she skipped aside and ran away. Gus took off after her and, once they were both gone, Harmony appeared.

Minutes later, she found what she was looking for: a container marked PLASTIC EXPLOSIVES. A snort made her turn. Grunter was standing in the doorway.

'I've got the evidence. It was Gus.'

'Snurf snort gruntle,' said Grunter, which meant, 'It's a fair cop, guv.'

That evening Aunt Glenda, accompanied by Harmony and Dino, took the incriminating box to the Grobbler caravan. Mr Grobbler looked shell-shocked. Gus stood to one side, his eyes cast down, looking at the floor.

'I can't believe it. I just can't believe it. My own boy. My own innocent little Augustus, sweet as a cherub and twice as sugary. Say you didn't do it, boy,' Mr Grobbler said, close to tears.

'I didn't do it, Dad,' Gus said.

Mr Grobbler turned to Aunt Glenda appealingly. 'There! He denies it, and I ask you, look at those lips, lips what has never had an untruth pass between 'em. And those eyes. Eyes as was manufactured in Heaven and shoved in his bonce by angels.'

'Mr Grobbler, perhaps Gus is lying,' Aunt Glenda suggested.

Mr Grobbler turned to Gus. 'Gus, is you not what I think you is? Is you a poisoned chalice, a flower with a corrupt heart? Is you ambiguous, boy?'

'I dunno what you're on about,' Gus said truthfully. He often didn't know what his father was talking about.

'To speak plain, is you lying, boy? Did you blow up the dubree next door? The truth now,' Mr Grobbler said.

Gus looked up. 'It weren't my fault. They's always on at us, always getting me going,' he said.

'And now you got it comin'. It'll be prison for you and the cemetery for me after I die of a broken heart. Glenda, if I might call you that, you're a good neighbour and a fine woman. I even harboured a notion that you and me might . . .'

'Yes, I'm sure you did, but to get back to Gus,' Aunt Glenda said, looking embarrassed.

'A favour for a broken man. Let me and Augustus have one more night as father and son under the same roof and tomorrow you can take him down to the Old Bill,' Mr Grobbler said, wiping his runny eyes and nose with a dirty cuff.

'But . . . oh, all right. One night. We'll be here at nine to take Gus to the police,' Aunt Glenda said.

It was a night for revelations. Harmony and Dino sat in the hold sharing a chocolate swiss roll to celebrate the confirmation of Gus's guilt. As they were talking,

Harmony noticed a photograph poking out from Dino's tin of special things. She took it and Dino tried to snatch it back.

'Let's have a look,' Harmony said, holding the photograph out of Dino's reach.

Dino decided it couldn't do any harm. The photograph showed a man and a woman with three little girls, one no more than a baby.

'This is me,' Dino said, pointing to the smallest girl. 'These are my mum and dad . . . They . . . they died in a car crash. I don't know who the other two girls are'.

'Come with me,' Harmony said.

They went into Harmony's room. She opened a drawer and took out a photograph identical to the one Dino had. They held the two photos side by side. Dino looked amazed. Harmony pointed at the two older girls.

'This is me, aged three, and this is Melody,' Harmony said. She turned over the photograph. On the back someone had written 'Harmony, Melody, Sally, Auntie Helen & Uncle Frank'.

'Sally, but . . .' Dino's voice trailed off.

'Were you given another name after your parents died?' Harmony asked.

'I was only little. Maybe,' Dino said.

'Don't you see? We're cousins!' Harmony said.

It had to be true. Harmony had been told that, once her cousin Sally's parents had died, she had been taken abroad by an uncle. Dino scoffed at the mention of an uncle, but her mind was whirled round and round by the thought that she really did have a family, of sorts. She and Harmony stood side by side and looked in the mirror. Dino took off her cap and yes, there was a resemblance.

'Welcome home,' Harmony said. 'Thanks to the Queen's Nose.'

Dino needed time to collect her thoughts on her own, then she would tell Harmony . . . everything.

Dino walked along the towpath, absorbing the knowledge that she now had cousins, aunts, uncles, that she wasn't alone in the world. If only she'd known before that she had a family, everything could have been different. She wouldn't . . . Her thoughts were interrupted by shouts from the Grobbler caravan. Gus was begging his dad not to shop him, that he would go off his head in the nick, that there would be no one to look after Grunter. Dino listened and wanted to weep. Grunter approached her and she bent to stroke him.

'Gruntle, grunt, grunt,' he said, which meant, 'I know he's a lost cause, but the kid's all I got.'

Perhaps Dino understood what Grunter was saying, or perhaps it was the discovery of who she was that opened a door in her heart to the idea that Gus, Mr Grobbler and Grunter were a family, or perhaps it was because she didn't want to be questioned too closely by the police herself – whatever the reason, she took out the Queen's Nose and wished.

'I know Gus and his dad are a couple of old donkeys but I wish that . . . Glenda and Melody would love them, big time, so all this police stuff gets dropped. Is that clear?'

A low rumble of thunder seemed to answer her, then the sky purpled and lightning flashed.

'Blimey,' said Dino, and Grunter agreed.

CHAPTER 10

Melody sat at the table drumming her fingers. She had a recording session at ten o'clock that morning. Aunt Glenda was supposed to be taking Gus to the police station at nine, then coming back and giving Melody a lift. It was already a quarter to ten. She'd be late. Now she would have to go to that disgusting caravan to find out what had happened. It was all such a nuisance, the way people let you down. If only everyone could be kind and unselfish like her, she thought, as she tottered in her high-heeled boots across the scrapyard to the filthy old caravan.

As she approached the caravan she could hear laughter and giggling coming from inside. One voice sounded like Aunt Glenda's, but it was more girlish, and Aunt Glenda didn't usually indulge in high-pitched, girly giggling. The other voice was much stranger. At first she thought it was Mr Grobbler's, but then it sounded like some sort of large animal: a laugh that became the *eeh-awh* braying of an ass.

Melody opened the door and entered, recoiling instantly at the powerful animal smell, like that of a badly kept stable which hadn't been cleaned for months. She followed the giggling and stopped, speechless, at the sight before her.

Mr Grobbler was lying on a hammock, munching loudly first from a plate of chips then on a large brown carrot which he kept dipping in a bowl of brown sauce. Bottles of brown ale were strewn around on the carpet. But this was not the Mr Grobbler Melody had come to know and be disgusted by – he was much worse. His facial features had become distorted so that they resembled those of an ass rather than a man. His ears had grown longer and had bushy tufts of hair sprouting from them. His cheeks were hairy and he had grown large, yellowing, tobacco-stained teeth, with copious amounts of saliva around his chops. His hands were covered in hair and his nails were blackened to hoof colour. He had also grown a tail, which sprouted through his trousers. The smell that came from him was awesome.

Rather than being repelled, Aunt Glenda was kneeling by the hammock, stroking Mr Grobbler's long ears and weaving daisies in his tail. Every now and then she puckered up and planted little kisses on his hairy forehead with much dove-ing and cooing. Melody could tell instantly that this was a woman seriously in love. It was disgusting. It was inexplicable.

Mr Grobbler gave a loud belch which shook the caravan. 'Needed that, better out than in, *eeh awh*!' he said, his voice a strange nasal whine that often ended in a bray, as if something in him couldn't decide whether he was human or ass.

Aunt Glenda laughed. 'Oh, George, you're a caution. The wit just pours from you,' she said.

'What are you doing with that thing, Aunt Glenda?' Melody asked, finding her voice at last.

Aunt Glenda turned her glazed love-struck eyes towards Melody. 'I'm ministering to my love's needs. His every whim. His smallest desire. Look at those eyes, those teeth, that noble jaw. To kiss these blessed hairy chops. Just to look makes me weak at the knees.'

Melody was growing weak in the stomach. 'How can you? He is gross. And I can smell him from here, he's . . .'

She stopped in her tracks as Gus entered. He hobbled rather than walked, given that the ends of his legs were now more like hooves than feet. His face too had been peculiarly rearranged so that he looked ass-like, with a longish snout and hairy ears. He had a finger in one ear and was trying to extract something, either a bug or a dirt ball. But Melody only saw someone she had been waiting for all her life, the realization of every romantic dream she'd ever had.

'. . . a dream come true. Gus. Darling,' she said.

Gus looked around, assuming that Melody meant some other Gus, but there was only him.

'Wot's up with you?' he asked in a nasal *eeh awh* voice.

'Nothing. Everything is wonderful. Just don't let this be an illusion, Gus, say you're real,' she begged.

Gus gave a huge bray and an *eeh awhshoooooo* sneeze, spraying Melody with things no human being should ever be sprayed with. Her face was covered with slime and snotty substances. She wiped it blissfully.

'You are real! My love, let me wipe your wonderful snout.' And Melody wiped the snotty snout of Gus with her sleeve.

Looking at Gus and Melody together, Mr Grobbler had an uneasy feeling that something else ought to be happening, something to do with the police; but Aunt Glenda soon soothed away his worries with kisses and another glass of brown ale.

Harmony was returning to the boat after doing a few pet therapy sessions at the Centre when Grunter came running up to her.

'Hello, boy, what's up?' she said, stroking his snout.

'Grurf gruntle snurf!' Grunter said, meaning, 'It's not a pretty sight!'

'Come on, boy, show me what it is,' she said.

'Snurf gruntle,' meaning, 'Better take a sick bag.'

Harmony had to rub her eyes to make sure it was really happening. There was Mr Grobbler, or something that vaguely resembled Mr Grobbler, in a hammock on the boat deck, with Aunt Glenda tickling his feet and both of them laughing and giggling. A similarly transformed Gus was in a deck chair with Melody spooning cold baked beans into his mouth from a large bucket.

Harmony didn't know whether to laugh or cry. It was both fascinating and appalling. The two couples were so engrossed in each other they didn't even notice her as she walked past them. Something had gone seriously wrong, and it didn't take a genius to work out who was probably behind it. Dino just didn't know when to leave things alone. Harmony went downstairs to find her.

Dino was in the kitchen. She had a photograph pinned to a wall and she was throwing a dart at it, then another and another. She took the darts out and threw them again. She was angry and not a little frightened. She gazed at the photograph of a man with long reddish hair and narrow blue eyes that gleamed with pure malice.

'What are you doing?' Harmony asked.

Dino turned guiltily and tore down the photograph. 'Nothing,' she said.

'That was Aunt Glenda's photograph. From her crime folder. How do you know that bloke?'

'I don't. I just . . . leave me be!' Dino said.

Harmony decided to let the matter drop for now. The most pressing concern was Melody and Aunt Glenda.

'It was you, wasn't it? You wished for them to fall in love,' she asked.

Dino grinned. 'Yeah. Cool, eh?'

'No. Not cool at all. Listen, we're going to have to put up with the Grobblers all the time, so we'll be the ones to suffer. And when Mum and Dad come back, they'll go ballistic when they find their drippy daughter snogging a donkey,' Harmony said.

Dino refused to use another wish. She had only three left and wasn't going to waste them on other people any more. Whenever she tried to help it went wrong, so the last wishes were for her, and that was final. At least, she thought it was. Then Melody, Gus, Aunt Glenda and Mr Grobbler came clomping downstairs. Aunt Glenda was carrying two bottles of champagne and she popped the cork from one of them.

'Aren't you going to congratulate us?' Melody asked, stroking Gus's head lovingly.

'Why?' Harmony asked.

'Gus and I are going to get married,' Melody said excitedly.

'And so are George and I,' Aunt Glenda said.

'Gus and I will have loads of babies. I hope they all have his looks,' Melody said.

'So – looks like you and us is going to be family, young Harmony. All snug as bugs, close as fleas on a dog's bottom. Hee haw!' Mr Grobbler brayed.

Harmony was stunned.

Dino was astonished.

'When is this . . . I mean . . . when?' Harmony asked feebly.

'This afternoon. We've got special licences,' Aunt Glenda said.

And the two happy couples left to arrange their wedding outfits. Harmony and Dino were to be bridesmaids, which horrified the two girls even more as it meant wearing posh frocks.

'This is serious,' Harmony said.

Dino agreed. She got her special tin and took out the book and the coin. She rubbed the Queen's Nose and wished. 'I wish that those disgusting Grobblers, and Melody and Glenda will fall out of love.'

The pages of the book fluttered and stopped at a blank page. Slowly, as they watched, the face of Uncle Ginger materialized, surrounded by clouds which occasionally drifted across his face.

'Uncle Ginger. You know what's happened?' Harmony asked.

'Of course,' he replied. 'And I'm afraid you are both going to have to work a bit harder to solve this one. Use your wits as well as your wishes. And don't always think in straight lines, because things don't always go from A to B to C. Think sideways or backwards sometimes – it's good exercise for the mind. This might help.'

His face disappeared and was replaced by a rhyme:

> *Richard Elbborg as a name is strange;*
> *Say it shortly thrice to change.*
> *But transformations are nasty tricks;*
> *So find a final cure in volix.*

97

Harmony wrote it down. Neither she nor Dino could make any sense of it. They would have to work it out though, and pretty soon, because the wedding was only three hours away.

At ten to three the strange little band were gathered outside the Register Office, waiting for their turn. Grunter was there as Mr Grobbler's best man, with a little black bow-tie around his neck, which he had decided to eat as soon as he could get it off. Harmony was wearing a pink bridesmaid's dress which she privately vowed she would cut into shreds and burn as soon as she could. 'Richard Elbborg as a name is strange; Say it shortly thrice to change.' She kept saying Richard Elbborg, Richard Elbborg, Richard Elbborg as the rhyme had suggested, but nothing happened. Time was running out for them to do something to stop this nightmare.

They were ushered in and walked up to the desk behind which stood the Superintendent Registrar. He looked up from his papers and took a little involuntary jump back in fright.

'Ah, ah, ah, I . . .' he fumbled for words.

'Cough it up, boy. Have a good spit,' Mr Grobbler said. 'That's what I always does to clear the tubes,' and he spat into a flower vase on the table.

The Registrar gave a nervous little laugh, dabbed beads of sweat from his nose and forehead, then he saw Grunter. 'Is that, is that a . . . ?' he began.

'*Certainment*. My best man. Even coming on the honeymoon,' Mr Grobbler said.

'Grunt gruntle gruntle,' Grunter said, meaning, 'I'm a pig, not a gooseberry!'

The Registrar managed to control his hysteria and began the service. As his voice droned on, Harmony felt increasingly desperate. She couldn't believe the Queen's Nose would let this happen. Perhaps the coin was fed up with her and Dino; or perhaps the magic had gone wrong.

Then she noticed a sign on the Registrar's desk:

SUPERINTENDENT REGISTRAR
MR A. NERVEWINKLE

'A. Nervewinkle,' Harmony whispered. 'That's it! The rhyme said to shorten, and how do you shorten a name? You abbreviate the first name. So Richard Elbborg is . . .'

'R. Elbborg,' Dino said.

'Relbborg,' Harmony said, her mind now racing, 'and Uncle Ginger said to think backwards too, so Relbborg is . . . Grobbler!'

'Right. Say it three times like the rhyme told you to,' Dino hissed excitedly.

'Grobbler Grobbler Grobbler!' Harmony said.

Suddenly everything seemed to slow down and the voice of the Registrar became a low, deep drone, each word taking an age to happen. The room shimmered and there was a pulse in it, like a giant heartbeat.

Nothing seemed to be in focus, and as Harmony looked around she noticed that something odd was happening to the Grobblers: their old selves were starting to reassert themselves, the ass-like features shrinking and changing, but then the pulse weakened and their features became ass-like again. The shimmering stopped. The Registrar spoke normally. It hadn't worked. This awful farce of a double wedding was going ahead after all.

'It's no good, we need the second part of the riddle,' Harmony said.

'"But transformations are nasty tricks, So find a final cure in volix." Volix? Is that a proper word?' asked Dino.

'No. I looked it up. Think! I got the last clue from his name. There must be a clue to the second part around here,' Harmony said desperately.

They both searched everywhere with their eyes as the service progressed. Fairly soon both Melody and Aunt Glenda would be married to two human monsters.

'Nothing I can see. Not even any words, except for them,' Dino said, indicating an 'Order of Service' chart on the wall.

Harmony read it several times over, searching for clues:

i.   Enter in silence
ii.   Remain seated until you are asked to stand
iii. Repeat the exact words of the registrar
iv.   After the service be seated while the register is signed

Nothing there, she thought, unless . . . that was it!

'Got it!' Harmony said.

Melody turned and shushed her.

'It's not the words, it's the numbers. Roman numerals,' Harmony said. 'It isn't volix, it's volume nine: vol. ix – one followed by x.'

'Oh, I could have got that dead easy,' Dino said loftily.

'Sure,' Harmony said. 'Now, you hold things up.'

'Where are you going?' Dino asked.

'To find volume nine.'

Harmony raced out. Beneath the dress she had leggings and a T-shirt on, so as she ran she ripped off the dreaded dress.

Her mind was going like a greyhound when, a few minutes later, she bounded up the steps of the public library. Volume nine, but volume nine of what? Wishes? Trouble? Magic? She ran along the shelves until she found a section on magic. There was only one collection, called 'A Guide to Magic', with more than nine volumes. She took down volume nine and looked through the chapter headings. One chapter was entitled 'Transformations'. She flipped the pages and read the sub-headings: people into insects, objects, reptiles, animals. She turned to the animal section and came to a page that mentioned asses and donkeys. As she started to read, the words dropped to the bottom of the page and disappeared, to be replaced by another riddle:

2 of H and one of O
Will reinstate the status quo.

She raced out of the library, repeating the riddle over and over to herself.

The marriage ceremony was almost concluded. The Registrar asked all those present to stand to witness the solemn moment when the marriage contract would be signed.

'You can't!' Dino shouted.

'I'm sorry?' the Registrar asked. 'Is there some legal reason why these four people cannot be married?'

'Er, yes,' Dino said.

'Shut up, Dino, and let him get on with it,' Aunt Glenda said.

'But . . . but Mr Grobbler's already married. In fact he's been married fifteen times. He's a . . . wotsit . . . a bigamist!' Dino lied.

An awful row started and Mr Grobbler grabbed the Registrar by the lapels and told him to get on with his job. Melody shouted at Dino. Grunter ate the flowers.

Harmony raced up the steps chanting the riddle – then it came to her: two of H and one of O was H_2O. Water!

As she ran into the Register Office a man was cleaning the windows. Harmony grabbed his bucket of water and went straight in. Everyone turned towards her.

'Not you spoiling my day, too!' Melody screamed.

And with a feeling of no little satisfaction, Harmony emptied the bucket of water over the two happy couples and shouted, 'Grobbler! Grobbler! Grobbler!'

The room trembled. Pictures shook. The Grobblers' faces twisted and turned as their features returned to normal. Aunt Glenda and Melody slowly calmed down and started to look around in amazement. Things were back to something like normal.

Harmony took Dino's arm and led her away from the bewildered little band. She suddenly felt very tired and wanted to be in the fresh air. Outside the building, her energy started to come back, so she turned to Dino and said, 'Race you to the bus stop!' and she was off.

Dino was about to give chase when a voice behind her chilled her to the marrow.

'Hello, Jellybean. I've been lost without you. But not for much longer, eh?'

Even before she turned around she knew that the past had caught up with her and that her life would never be the same again. She could never escape.

CHAPTER 11

His name was Daniel Block. He had been Dino's guardian, and after the death of her parents he told her that she had no other family, which was a lie. He was very good at getting to know down-and-out children who had nowhere else to go, then involving them in criminal activities. He taught then shoplifting, burglary and snatching handbags and, like many powerful personalities, once the children were under his control they found it impossible to get away from him. It was unwise to cross him. Dino had been the exception, and it had nagged and nagged at Block until he could think of nothing else but getting her back. She was his only failure, and she would return to him or else.

Daniel Block was also a disappointed man. He felt that the world should have rewarded his intelligence and talents without all this struggle. The world had let him down, and the more he felt this the more he lost touch with it. Sometimes he woke up in the night knowing that something had slipped in his mind, some important cog. Whereas most people would be terrified by this, he was intrigued, amused. As a teenager he had been graceful and athletic, and there was still something elegant about him, as if he were a fallen angel. He was also dangerous to know and he was after Dino. He'd made that clear.

Harmony and Dino were on the bus. Harmony listened, fascinated, as Dino told her about her former criminal life with Block. In a way Harmony envied her. As a story it all sounded dangerous and romantic, but Harmony knew that the reality must have been a nightmare. Dino also said that Block often kept the children hungry, because he thought hunger was a great motivator.

'Why didn't you just run away?' Harmony asked.

'You don't know him. He's powerful. Anyway, once you've done a few jobs then you're a criminal. It gives him more power over you 'cos he can shop you. He's the bloke in the photograph that Aunt Glenda has, so the police must be after him. But if they get him, he'll tell them about me too. I'm scared, Harm.'

Block had told Dino to meet him that evening by the canal bridge at eight o'clock. Dino had decided that she would go and would tell no one. She had rediscovered a family and she didn't want to get them into trouble, so it seemed better just to give in to Block. After supper she packed a few things in a battered case and slipped away from the boat.

She had reckoned without Harmony Parker, though. Harmony had guessed that there was something Dino had kept from her, so she was waiting for her on the towpath.

'Push off, Harmony. You're different to me, with your poncey voice and your family and all the stuff you won – CDs, guitar and stuff. My world's different and I don't want you in it,' Dino said.

'Too bad, 'cos you're stuck with me,' Harmony retorted, too clever by half to be fooled by Dino's attempt at rejection. 'You can go back only if you agree to my plan.'

Aunt Glenda was furious. 'You just let her go back to this man Block? Do you have any idea how dangerous he is?' she said.

'She's going to let me know where she is, then we can catch Block,' Harmony said.

'And how is she going to contact you?' Aunt Glenda asked.

'I gave her a mobile phone.'

'And where did you get that from?'

'Your handbag,' Harmony said.

Dino was sitting on some old sacks in a large disused warehouse somewhere along the canal. It was dark, dirty, oily and full of ropes, pulleys and rusting industrial equipment. Block was sitting on a crate picking his teeth with a long metal pin. 'Like the gaff, Jellybean? The Café Royal of the canal,' he said.

'It's a rat hole. Which is why you're here, I s'pose,' Dino said.

Block tut-tutted. Being away from him had given Dino a little independence and freedom of thought which, he knew, were dangerous things. They breed discontent. He'd soon stamp that out. Like a cat and without any warning he grabbed a microphone from a box, jumped up and pulled a switch on a panel. Disco lights flashed on and off and his voice resonated through loudspeakers as he sang: 'Anarchy and unrest are in very bad taste So we'll have to teach Dino to know her place.' He smiled at Dino. 'Like the gear? A famous disc-jockey left it in his Ferrari. I could have been a star myself, don't you think, Jellybean? A star with a very large car.'

'You're nuts,' Dino said.

'And you're back,' Block replied.

The next morning Harmony was trying to share her anxieties about Dino with Gregory, but he was only half listening as he fiddled with a new invention of his for the Garden Centre – a small chip that gave out sonic vibrations to attract insects. A lot of plants were being eaten by insects, and the plan was that this device, placed just outside the Garden Centre, would therefore keep them outside. He could even operate it with a handset remote control.

'So maybe Aunt Glenda's right and I shouldn't have let her go. What do you think, Grogsy?' Harmony asked.

He wasn't listening. 'I think this little baby is just about perfect.'

The telephone rang and Harmony answered. It was Dino to say she was all right. The idea was to try to get Block to trust her again in order to make it easier to trap him. The trouble was, he was too clever for that to work straight away; it would take time. Harmony told her to stay cool and ring again that evening. When she hung up, Harmony thought that the whole idea of letting Dino go back to Block had probably been a mistake, but for now there wasn't much she could do about it, except worry.

Block took Dino out early next morning to a department store where they were going to work a familiar routine. Dino would bump into a woman, knocking her bags on to the floor, and Block would help the woman retrieve her shopping, using the opportunity to remove her purse. It usually worked well, but Dino was out of practice and was also incredibly nervous. For a moment she thought of just running, but Block would find her, just as he had found her before. And if she just screamed for the police he would find some way of getting back at her, or at Harmony and the others. The two of them just managed to get out of the store before the woman noticed that her purse was gone.

Block dragged Dino back to the warehouse. He was

not happy. 'Don't ever shop me, Jellybean. I'm all you've got,' he said.

'I've got friends. And family,' Dino said defiantly.

Block scoffed at the idea. 'The Parkers. They were just using you to get at me. That Glenda woman had my photograph, and you can bet she knew all about you. If they had got me, they would have dumped you like a piece of scrap. You didn't really think it was because of some inner quality in you, did you? Some little bit of stardust they loved in you. Oh no. Now – tell me about the Queen's Nose,' he said.

'I dunno what you're on about,' Dino said.

'Jellybean, don't make me angry, because when I'm angry everything starts to shimmer and I have visions. Visions of fire and glass.'

He threw a bottle at a wall and it shattered. Then he took a little red book out of his pocket.

'I've read your diary, so I know. Now. Tell me. The Queen's Nose.'

Dino told him all about the Queen's Nose, and it fired his imagination. He knew there were things in this world stranger than truth and his often bored and restless mind seized on all the possibilities that something like the Queen's Nose had to offer. He wanted it so much that it started to blur his judgement. Dino had deliberately left the coin on the boat, so there was no chance of Block taking it, but now he wanted it very badly. He told Dino what they were going to do.

Later that afternoon, Block had the disco lights flashing and he was playing an electric guitar at full volume so that the warehouse shook with sound. Dino was convinced he was going out of his mind as he whirled and twirled in his own private concert.

She crept into a corner and telephoned Harmony. 'He wants me to steal the Queen's Nose. Tonight. In return, he says I can come back to you. Yes, of course he's lying, but what can I do? OK. Tonight.'

Harmony put down the phone and immediately started making plans. She was going to get this Block character. With a bit of help.

That night Harmony and Gregory were in the hold, waiting. At about one thirty the hatch opened and Dino entered.

'Are you all right?' Gregory asked.

'If you call staying with a criminal nutter in a stinking warehouse all right, then, yes, I'm fine.'

Harmony took the fifty-pence piece from her pocket and gave it to Dino. They had a plan worked out: Aunt Glenda had arranged for a plain-clothes policeman to follow Dino so that if Block didn't let her go, he could be arrested for kidnap as well as his other crimes. Harmony and Gregory were going to the warehouse so that they would be waiting too, ready to telephone the police when Block came back with Dino.

Dino was still unsure. She knew how smart he was. 'If only we had some sort of tracker device,' she said.

'Something like this?' Gregory said, producing his insect chip.

'But that's to attract insects!' Harmony said.

'Better than nothing,' Gregory said, feeling slightly hurt.

Dino took the little microchip and left.

Block was waiting outside.

She gave him the coin. 'Can I go now?' she asked.

'Of course you can't, Jellybean, but then we both knew that,' he said, taking her arm and leading her off into the night. Moments later, a figure in a raincoat and trilby hat emerged from the shadows to follow them.

Block had no intention of going back to the warehouse where Dino might have arranged for someone to be waiting. He had a new hiding-place under some railway sidings, near the gasometer. They had to climb down a ladder to get inside, so it was impossible to see from outside.

When they had got inside, Block took the mobile phone out of Dino's pocket and crushed it beneath his heel. 'It's not good to talk,' he said. Then he took out the coin and held Dino's hand to make her rub the Queen's Nose. He thought that probably she had to be the one to rub the coin, but there was no reason why he shouldn't wish on her behalf.

'Dino wishes that Harmony Parker will be destroyed by . . . let's see, earth, air, fire, water. Yes, by water,' he said.

'No!' Dino said.

CHAPTER 12

Block eventually fell asleep and the fifty-pence piece glittered on the floor beside him, where it had fallen out of his pocket. He had tied Dino's hands together, then tied them to a post, so it was useless to think of escape – that is, until she saw a figure in a raincoat and trilby hat climb quietly through a window. So a detective had tracked them after all! Dino's heart leapt. Then the detective took off the trilby hat – and it was Aunt Glenda. Dino almost cried out in despair but managed to stop herself. Aunt Glenda untied Dino's hands, then pointed to the ladder which led up to the door. They climbed up and got outside.

Aunt Glenda beamed. 'I shall promote myself to Chief Detective for this,' she said proudly.

'Hang on. I forgot something,' Dino said, and, before Aunt Glenda could stop her, Dino had gone back.

She approached the sleeping Block and picked up the Queen's Nose, then she carefully put Gregory's tiny transmitter in one of his pockets. She turned to go, but when her foot was on the second rung of the ladder a hand grabbed her from behind and a voice hissed: 'Whatever I do now, Jellybean, it's your fault.'

Two minutes later a worried-looking Aunt Glenda

came back down the ladder. Dino was lying on the floor gagged and tied to a wooden post. When Aunt Glenda reached the ground Block jumped out from behind some sacking and grabbed her.

'You deranged . . . !' Her words were cut off as Block stuffed a gag in her mouth and then stuck tape over it. He dragged her outside towards the water-filled gasometer. She looked over the rim. A ladder led down into the deep, cold water. Block made her climb a little way down the ladder, then he tied a rope around her. Next, he looped the rope under the ladder and tied the other end to the working gasometer. As the gasometer rose, so the rope would slowly pull Glenda under the water. It would be a slow and interesting death, he thought. Not many people came by, so he reckoned she had a one-in-ten chance of escaping.

A sudden noise made him turn: Dino had managed to break free and was looking down in horror at Aunt Glenda. Block left Glenda to her death and made a grab for Dino, who turned and ran like the wind. Even as he left, the water in the gasometer started to rise.

Harmony and Gregory waited for hours until it became clear that Block and Dino were not going to return to the warehouse. They decided to split up and search in different areas. Harmony was going to work along the canal in one direction and Gregory in the other. As Gregory set off, he took his insect remote-control device from his pocket. He pressed the button on it and thought that Harmony had been right – it was stupid to think it would be useful.

In fact, it was extremely fortunate that Gregory did press the button at that precise moment. Dino was running for all she was worth along the canal towpath, but Block was gaining on her and was just about to reach out and grab her when he suddenly had to slow down as black flies and midges started to attack his face and hands. Within moments he was covered in a stinging, buzzing, biting insect army.

Dino stopped and watched, breathless, from a distance. Block was flapping and waving the insects away when he either fell, or perhaps dived, into the canal. He vanished under the dirty, oily surface and the waters closed over him. Apart from a little backwash it was as if he had never been.

Dino approached, tentatively, and stared down, but the water was too polluted to see anything but the oily mirrored surface.

Then through the reflection of her face a hand thrust up out of the water and grabbed her ankle. She almost fell in herself as Block heaved himself up and on to the bank, gasping in great lungfuls of air. He held on to Dino while he stood and shook himself like a dog. His eyes gleamed like blue steel. 'You must have been so worried for me,' he said.

'I wish you'd drowned,' Dino said.

'You don't mean that. Now let me show you my other residence. Open sesame,' he said, as he bent down and lifted a drain cover on the towpath.

Dino looked down into the darkness. A sewer. She resisted as Block tried to push her down.

'Why are women so difficult to please?' he said as he shoved her down the metal ladder and then followed her down himself, pulling the cover back into place behind him.

Minutes later, Harmony came running along. She stopped at the wet patch on the path and looked at the confusion of footprints. She saw the drain cover and lifted it. It's dark, it stinks, I can't go down there, she thought. But she knew she had to, and after a moment's hesitation she descended the metal steps.

Everywhere there were echoes and dripping and strange little noises that could have been rats. Harmony stopped every now and then to listen as she trudged through the slime and muck in the sewer. Then she saw a light dancing ahead, slowly coming towards her. She found a niche in the wall and pressed herself into it, waiting. Block had a torch and he was dragging Dino along. He was wet and filthy, and he was becoming increasingly deranged; he even seemed to be enjoying what was happening in a mad sort of way. He was singing at the top of his voice: 'Singing in the drain, Just singing in the drain.' He stopped singing as a thought entered his twisted mind. 'Jellybean, you are just not entering into the spirit of this. Isn't this wonderful? Isn't it perfect? Aren't you just having the most glorious time?' he asked.

Harmony jumped out and faced them.

'Harm!' Dino said.

'The illustrious Harmony Parker, I assume. A pleasure to meet you,' Block said.

'Dino never told me how ugly you are. Won any competitions for it?' Harmony asked.

Block smiled.

'Jellybean, I don't think I approve of your little friend.'

'Harm, he wished, with the Queen's Nose, that you'd be destroyed by water!' Dino said.

'I cannot tell a lie. I did. Please forgive me, it was all done in fun,' Block said sarcastically.

Harmony suddenly lashed out with her foot and kicked the torch flying from Block's hand, sending it splashing into the muck. Harmony bent down and grabbed it. Block slipped as he tried to snatch the torch back.

Dino gave him a sharp boot in the shins as he got to his feet.

'Quick! Run!' Harmony shouted.

The two girls ran, splashing and slipping, through the pipe.

Moments later Block was after them.

At times it seemed they were getting away, then he

would be there again, gaining on them, becoming madder and more deranged as he did so. 'Wait for me, girls! I want to play too!' he shouted.

This guy is seriously, frighteningly nuts, Harmony thought as she ran.

Eventually Dino stopped. 'I can't carry on! Stitch. You go,' she said, holding her side.

The girls stopped and turned. Block was about five metres away.

He stopped and smiled. 'Come to Daddy,' he said.

'What do you want?' Harmony asked.

The question seemed to surprise Block. His face became serious, almost pleading, like a little lost boy.

'I want . . . everything,' he said.

Somewhere, far off, a slow roar began, like a distant wave.

'The Queen's nose can give you everything. All your dreams, all the things you've imagined, everything you've envied. All yours,' Harmony said.

'I believe, I believe,' Block said. 'But will the magic work for little old me?' He felt in his coat pocket.

The coin was gone. Dino held it up.

Harmony took it from her. 'You can have it. Just let us go,' she said.

The roar was coming closer. Closer.

'No can do. Give me the coin and I promise I'll make it quick for you both. You'll only feel enough pain to make it fun for me,' Block said.

'Look!' Dino said, pointing to where a torrent of water was hurtling through the pipe. In a few moments it would be on them.

'Take it, then!' Harmony said, and she threw the coin towards the approaching water.

Block had a moment to decide whether to try to save himself or to go for the coin. He chose the coin and ran towards it as the oncoming water engulfed him, knocking him off his feet and sweeping him away like a doll. For a moment a hand was visible clutching the coin, then it was gone.

Harmony grabbed a metal ladder and hung on for dear life. She gripped Dino's hand and clung on to it tightly as the water hit them. Dino's hand almost slipped away, but she managed to swing round and grab the ladder too.

A few minutes later a drain cover was pushed up on the towpath and a bedraggled Harmony and Dino emerged. Mr Grobbler and Gus were sitting there, fishing, despite the fact that there were no fish in the canal. They both gaped at the two girls as they squelched past them. The girls ignored the Grobblers. They were too tired.

'Shame about the coin,' Dino said.

'You mean this,' Harmony said, producing the real Queen's Nose coin.

'You mean the other one wasn't the real Queen's Nose?'

''Course not,' Harmony said, grinning.

Dino's face turned white as she suddenly remembered Aunt Glenda. 'Oh no!' she said. 'Aunt Glenda! She'll be . . .' and off she ran, closely followed by Harmony.

But Glenda hadn't drowned. Gregory had found her while he was looking for Dino. She had realized, while she was in the tank, that one of the things she would miss if she drowned would be Dino. This surprised her, as she told Dino when she asked if she'd like to stay on the boat – permanently. While they were having their first argument about who would do the cooking Daniel Block emerged from a sewage pipe a few miles away, half dead, but alive enough to be aware of the blue uniforms around him, of the handcuffs and the speed of the police car which drove him to the station, and from there a long spell in prison.

Uncle Ginger paid a real visit, and he and Harmony went for a walk along the canal. They found a money-box bottle on the towpath.

'Look as if it's waiting for a message,' said Uncle Ginger.

Harmony understood. She took the Queen's Nose coin from her pocket and put it in the bottle. Uncle Ginger took a tiny notebook with a pencil from his back pocket and Harmony wrote in it: Ten Wishes. Use with Care. She folded the piece of paper and put it into the bottle, then used rolled leaves to plug the hole. She held it for a moment then threw the bottle into the canal. It sank, then bobbed up and started to float along quite fast, as if pushed by an invisible hand. It felt strange to Harmony to let the Queen's Nose go again, but somehow right. Sometimes you had to let things go, and if you did, they had a funny way of coming back again.

Uncle Ginger put the notebook back in his pocket and smiled as he produced a wad of papers from his other pocket. Harmony couldn't belive it. They were airline tickets for all of them to go to Australia.

After all, families shouldn't be apart for too long.